Through the Eyes
of a Servant

Published on Amazon 2023

First edition: November 2023

Independently published

ISBN: 9798863584379

Author: Priya Rohella

Editor: Jack Havver

Cover Illustration: Ritika Rohella

Contributors: Melissa Arslan, F. Jeewa, Livia Dabbs

Contents

Preface

Through the Eyes of a Servant is based on a reoccurring dream the author had for years. The image of a manor-house surrounded by a forest, a butler standing in a hallway, half obscured in darkness, followed by a lady entering an antique shop called *Bridgedale*. These were the roots of the plot, the vision of the author and soon, the inspiration for an entire story. A map of the Ethel's manor was also drawn up from remnants of the dream.

Much like the contributors who worked on the plot, every character in the book lives somewhere in England and their dialects reflect that. Notice how Paula and Thomas speak in sensitive Received Pronunciation, prim and at times, laid on a bit thick. Clement speaks with a clumsy, almost lost cockney accent, replacing 'you' for 'ya' and his favourite lexicon: 'Mate!' Cliffe's dialect is most enjoyable; his stuttering combined with his Geordie accent provides a stimulating challenge. The coachman replaces 'I' for 'Ah' and 'well' for 'whey', keep up with it and you too will see how enjoyable it can be.

Besides from dialect, there are also a few other things to note. *Stone-Arch bridge* was inspired by the old tales of London Bridge, where supposedly, Victorian children would be forced under the structure, their bodies slowly decomposing, their bones left behind to fill the eroding intervals leading to sections of the bridge collapsing. The workhouses mentioned too, reflect the grim reality of the Victorian era. Many orphans were left to die unless a wealthy patron could pay for their survival.

On a less grizzly note, it is recommended when reaching certain points of the book, music should be played to fully immerse yourself into the scene. Such scenes will be marked with a reference and *footnote* such as this one[1]. Footnotes are also included to explain various quirks not mentioned in the main story. Do enjoy your time with *Through the Eyes of a Servant...* can you deduce the identity of the killer before reading chapter eight?

---

[1] It's the quirky things that make a good book a good read.

Foreword

I've known the author for the best part of four years now and in those four years I have had the pleasure of watching her writing grow; from poetry to short stories and eventually, novels. She has always managed to enrapture readers, capturing my and everyone else's imaginations with the stories she weaves.

One day she surprised me, asking if I would like to initially proofread her latest work, the title you are currently reading. We have worked together on several different projects from collaborative poems, script writing, to my own prose, and after a bit of back and forth with ideas and suggestions, the author promoted me to editor. A daunting task, I thought, but one that has become earnestly rewarding.

I have thoroughly enjoyed working on, reading, and re-reading Miss Rohella's novel, taking me back to old London town at the height of Queen Victoria's reign, from the dazzling ballrooms and manor homes of England's nobility, to the seedy back alleys where spring-heels lay in wait and the cackles of the unfortunate and the mad ring out.

I hope that you also enjoy following young Paula Ethel and Thomas Fulton through the twists and turns of murder, romance, and what is expected of one's position in life, as much as I have editing each and every page.

And to the author, thank you for this opportunity to join you on your latest adventure and I look forward to crafting the next one.

J. Havver
Editor.

Acknowledgments

I want to thank all the wonderful tutors and professors at Birmingham City University who helped me to hone my craft in creative writing. Special thanks to my illustrator and editor, whose dedication and hard work made this book possible.

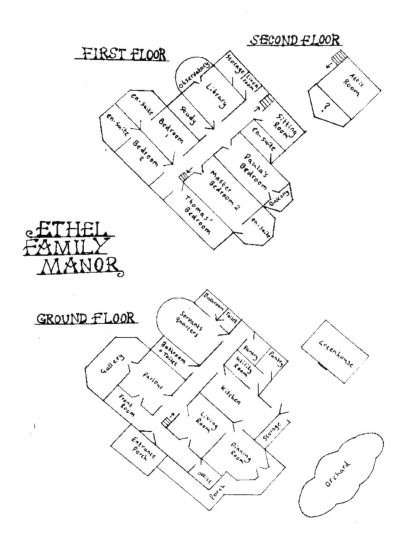

FIRST FLOOR

SECOND FLOOR

Observatory
Storage [linen] room
Library
Study
En-suite Bedroom
en-suite Bedroom 2
Sitting Room
En-suite
Palila's Bedroom
Balcony
Master Bedroom 2
Thomas' Bedroom
en-suite

Attic Room
?

ETHEL FAMILY MANOR

GROUND FLOOR

Bathroom Toilet
Servants Quarters
Pantry
Pantry
Utility Room
Greenhouse
Gallery
Bathroom + Toilet
Parlour
Kitchen
Front Room
Living Room
Storage
Entrance Porch
Dining Room
office
Orchard
Porch

9

Chapter 1

A Deadly mistake

Thomas Fulton, 24 years old, profession: butler. The intelligent, and somewhat sensitive man was born into a working-class family, fortunately, at a higher end than most unlucky souls. Since his youth he was fascinated with the upstanding nobles, duchesses and earls, always dreaming to meet them. Sadly, his father disapproved of his ambition of becoming a butler, believing the career only looked good on paper. Yet, despite his father's negative input, Thomas pursued his goals and found out first-hand what being a servant was all about.

Working full time as a butler was no easy feat for the man; it wasn't exactly how he envisioned it when he was younger. The hours were long, the holidays were scarce, but most of all, the isolation was enough to drive a sane man to *bedlam*. Thomas didn't really want to resign, but sometimes he dwelled upon the thought. His master, Earl Eric Randal, was an austere man who had his doubts about everyone, everyone except Thomas. Due to Randal's scepticism, the butler was the sole servant in the entire manor; the earl condemned anyone else to venture near his property, let alone prance inside.

In spite of all the negatives, the earl showered the butler with kindness and treated him more than fairly. Thus, was the reason, Thomas couldn't push himself to leave. Whenever his master wasn't busy directing his businesses, he always made time to play chess with the man. The two even mused over whisky in the dining hall on chilly winter evenings. Seeing his master happy was the greatest thing the butler could ever wish for.

"Fulton!"

At last his master was back from the workhouse. Thomas hurried along to the front room; Eric lounged on his velvet armchair, smoking a worn cigar. The man's eyes flicked up when his butler appeared.

"There you are, Fulton. What's your report for today?"

The butler's brows furrowed, but only for a second. "As standard as yesterday's, sir. The post arrived earlier on in the day, the milkman delivered two bottles, the paper boy rode past on schedule. No unauthorised individuals to report," he said.

The blonde man puffed grey smoke into the empty air, knocking the cigar's ash to the floor, "I see. Good."

Thomas stood there awkwardly for a moment. The two of them hadn't had a leisurely conversation in a while. It was always about reports or scouting out suspicious individuals around the estate. It was the norm for the earl, but Thomas wished his master would unwind for once. Just to break the tension between the two of them, the butler asked his master about his work.

"How was everything at the workhouse today, sir?" Thomas said.
Eric gave a mixed look of empathy and determination, "The number of arrivals has risen. There are more abandoned children and homeless individuals who need our help."

Thomas was staggered when he first found out about Randal's charitable hobbies. It's not often individuals of noble blood interacted with the underclasses, let alone help them, but Eric was...unique. On weekdays, the man would tend to his late father's confectionery business, and in his free time he would oversee and send donations to the local workhouse. It was true that people of his own stature disliked him, but that didn't matter to Randal. When Eric saw the carefree faces of the workhouse children, his purpose was fulfilled. At least they saw him as a saviour.

"You perform a great service, my lord."

Eric stared off into the distance, almost looking teary-eyed.

"One must fulfil the purpose he has been sent here to do, or as you say, preform his duty to the very end."

Eric gave the butler a small smile before taking another intoxicating puff of the dwindling cigar. Crushing the tip against the ashtray, he got up sluggishly, stopping at Thomas' side.

"I will have my evening tea at the usual time, for now I have some pressing work to get on with."

As Eric stood to take his leave, Thomas had the sudden urge to halt him in his tracks. The butler reached out an arm, but stopped himself from tapping the blonde's back.

Eric cocked his head over his shoulder, "Something the matter?"

Carefully choosing his next words, the butler hesitantly spoke.

"Do... do you need me to aid you with your paperwork?"

The man's forehead scrunched. His butler's reply seemed like it was fabricated on a whim, not at all what he really had on his mind. Eric caught sight of the clock; it was just passed five in the afternoon. The man wished he could enquire about Thomas' thoughts, but having little time on his hands, he simply brushed it off.

"I'll be fine. Thank you, Fulton."

The earl laid a hand on his butler's shoulder and gave a slight nod. Thomas watched his master leave, looking to the ashes on the floor. He didn't know why, but an odd feeling continued to prey on him. His master appeared different today, tired... clumsy, like he'd been working too vigorously and hadn't slept in days. The butler imagined he could question it later, perhaps when he brought Eric his tea. There were two hours before then, and the servant had a perplexing task to get on with.

Thomas went down to the cellar; he needed to reorganise the shelves and count the food supplies. As lengthy as the job was, it was all part of a butler's duty. It was both dusty and dingy in the cellar, a bit of cleaning needed to be conducted, but more-over, some natural light needed to grace the sandy concrete floor. The faint clicks of his pocket watch kept Thomas company. However, when he stopped by a barrel of red wine, he remembered how alone he was. Some of the rich, bloody liquid dripped from the barrel, pooling on the floor. There was an empty glass and an old newspaper on the tabletop nearby.

Thomas smiled to himself and whispered, "So this is where the master takes himself off to."

He skimmed the headline:

'Murder near St. James park!'

His brow furrowed. Crime was like a rabid dog, terrorising every nook of London. He prayed that one day all the suffering would end, and someone would stop all this madness. Sometimes he felt a reporter's career was far worse than any other. At least he wasn't exposed to such dastardly affairs.

While hauling jars of oats, and bottles of basil off the shelves, Thomas' hand grazed against something leathery. Cautiously bringing the object down, he realised he was holding an old scrapbook. The man let curiosity get the better of him. Flipping through the worn pages, he found the book was filled to the brim with photos of his master as a young lad.

There were pictures of Mr and Mrs Randal, pictures of Eric attired in posh suits, and a photograph of little Eric and a greyhound puppy. There were a few photographs of Eric in sport attire with another boy. A note was written beside it: *Archie Stitch and Eric Randal, promising in the world of horse racing.*

This book was such a cherished item, so why on earth was it left to rot in the cellar? The last page of the book depicted Eric, Eric's father, another well-dressed gentleman, and a little girl standing outside what looked like a teashop. Both men were shaking hands while holding onto the children; Eric had his father's hand tightly upon his shoulder, and the other gentleman was holding the small girl in his arms. Thomas inspected the photo closely; Eric had a shy grin on his face, he was staring at the girl. Was she his childhood sweetheart, perhaps? The butler shook his head and carefully placed the book back on the top shelf. It must have been placed there for some reason or another, so Thomas supposed he should leave it be.

After dusting the stringy cobwebs from the ceiling and sweeping the last ounces of dust off the floor, Thomas wiped his brow and took out his pocket watch. The time was at hand to prepare his master's evening appetisers. Making his way upstairs, the butler rolled up his sleeves and tied an apron over his waistcoat. Thomas worked furiously over the kitchen counter, measuring out cups of sugar and raisins for a batch of scones. He couldn't push the thoughts of Eric's strange behaviour out of his head. Was he tired? Under pressure? After some reasoning, Thomas concluded that his master must have been fatigued from staying up all night mending the window latches in his study. Honestly, the earl could have gotten him to fix it instead of piling more stress onto himself. But, as well as being unique, Eric was also quite the independent fellow.

The buttery aroma of dough put an end to Thomas' daydreams. He pulled the baked goods out of the oven and began plating them with jam and clotted cream, not forgetting about the pot of earl grey which had been brewing on the stove. He placed the scones and the cup of tea on a tray before gingerly walking to the earl's study.

The halls were nippy. "The fireplace must have burned out again," the butler mumbled as he treaded onwards. It may have just been his imagination, but the butler could have sworn he heard a whisper emanating from somewhere. When Thomas reached his master's door, he hesitated for a second, then knocked twice and waited to hear Eric's gruff voice to call in forth. It never came. He knocked again, thinking his master must have fallen asleep. But when a reply did not come, he entered the cold room. Thomas dropped the tray with a clatter. His master's head lay still at the desk. The window was wide open behind him, causing gusts of wind to cascade into the room.

Thomas felt increasingly nauseous as he got closer to the desk, witnessing the blood seeping from Eric's back and neck. He had been stabbed. Brutally, cruelly, his flesh was mangled, as if the assailant were drunk or stronger than three men put together. Eric's blonde hair was matted, red with his own blood, his pale skin also ruined to crimson. When seeing the earl's bloodshot eyes, the butler retched into his hands. They were unnaturally wide, and they were giving the butler a hellish stare. They were no longer the determined blue pupils Thomas used to know. Eric's expression lay frozen, as if the last thing he saw was enough to petrify his very soul, even in death.

Chapter 2

Signet Ring

In another manor, not too far off London town, a young lady read the paper aloud to her gardener. The two women were in a state of horror when they heard that Earl Randal was murdered in his own home.

"Such frightful business!" The scrawny blonde woman gasped as she accidentally flattened the newly bedded roses.

"It's just awful... Earl Randal had so many good years ahead of him too."

The young lady rolled up the newspaper, and gazed over the grassy hills. This was the fourth murder in two months! Whoever this notorious killer was, he clearly wasn't fond of the nobility. This made the young lady all the more anxious.

"If I may be so bold, my lady... I think hiring a butler would be in your best interest," said the gardener.

The young lady went silent. She knew she needed to find a butler soon. Having another servant around would lighten the workload for the others, and make life easier around the manor. But, unfortunately, she couldn't push herself to do it. Not since her old beloved butler passed away when she was only a child.

"With all the commotion going on these days, I just want you to be safe..."

The gardener spoke softly, looking up at the raven-haired girl with wide, round eyes. The young lady was just about to reply when-

"Paula dear!"

A woman wearing a red ribboned dress, long white gloves, and a purple signet ring, waved a welcoming hand from an oncoming carriage. As she left the carriage, her grey hair swayed in the autumn breeze. She opened her arms, showing a pearly grin.

"Grandmother Ophelia!"

Paula ran into her grandmothers' arms and embraced her tightly. After returning the squeeze, Ophelia held Paula at arm's length and admired her growing beauty.

"You remind me of your father."

The girl smiled and looked down at her feet. She did indeed resemble her father, the same curly black hair, the same deep blue eyes. The only trait she didn't share with her father was the courage to move forward.

"I need to discuss some matters with you, dear."

"Matters?"

The ambiguity of that sentence worried the girl; did she do something wrong? Her grandmother only gave a blank stare, and Paula took this as an indication to change her persona.

"Of course, grandmother. Please come inside."

Paula led her grandmother through the hallway and living room, careful not to walk in front of her. The fireplace in the dining room was roaring and the chandelier above illuminated the impressive paintings on the walls. The flames from the candelabras flickered silently, welcoming the matriarch to the near vacant manor-house. The two sat down at one end of the elegantly-carved oak table and waited for their food to be served. Paula felt guilty as her head chef, Clement Morris and her gardener and ever-present confidant, Christa Wood, took on all the household responsibilities on their own. If Paula weren't so fixated with the past, she could have hired a butler to aid them with the daily errands. How she wished she had the courage.

*

After a while of waiting, Clement and Christa entered the hall. They were each holding a plate of roast chicken, buttery vegetables, and casserole. Placing the steaming meals on the table, they bowed to take their leave. It was already unjust that they did so much manual labour, allowing them to take a break was the least Paula could do.

"Wait you two, please join us for dinner."
Before Paula could get out of her seat, her grandmother held out a hand.

"Paula, dear. While I admire your kindness, Clement and Christa must eat in their quarters, or perhaps the kitchen."
Paula felt a little disheartened at her grandmother's interjection but nodded.

"Off you go, you two," said Ophelia. The two servants stood and bowed, taking their leave. Paula often treated them like friends but they knew such behaviour wouldn't be entertained in front of older nobility.
Once the servants left, Paula started conversation, "How are you grandmother?"

The elderly lady adjusted the napkin on her lap before acknowledging her granddaughter's question.

"I'm as good as I can be Paula, things are quite relaxed in the countryside."

"It's nice to see you're taking it easy. How's grandfather?" Said Paula.

Ophelia unexpectedly giggled.

"Your grandfather's as lively as ever, he can't stop decorating the manor and garden. Honestly, I think he's enjoying it too much out there."

Paula was pleased her grandfather could finally relish his retirement. After years of running their tea company, he deserved to savour his idle time in peace. She had visited her grandparent's country house a few times, it was quaint and cosy, nothing like the intimidating manor Paula dwelled in.

"Your grandfather has always done things with his own two hands. Manual labour is something he knows all too well. Probably why he sympathises with his servants so much... just like you, Paula, dear."

Ophelia took miniscule bites of her lamb casserole, while surveying the dining room and her granddaughter. She noticed Paula had installed new textured wallpaper and had also hung a realistic floral painting, (which was a family heirloom), on the wall, matching the twilight hues of the room. After observing her granddaughter's ingenuity, she cleared her throat.

"So, my dear, how have you been these past few days? Did you manage to handle my responsibilities?"

"Of course, grandmother, I managed to carry out all the tasks you instructed me to."

For a few days, while Ophelia renovated the country house, she entrusted the manor to Paula. She wanted to get an idea of how much the girl could accomplish on her own, and was very proud to admit she was impressed. Paula managed to instruct the servants, check up on the family company and distribute funds to the workhouse, all while completing her own literature and piano lessons. Her grandmother's eyes glittered; she couldn't express how pleased she was.

"Are you alright, grandmother?"

"I'm fine my dear, just so very proud of you."

The servants listened behind the kitchen door, grinning at the sentiment; they were just as awestruck with Paula's leadership. Clement and Christa were apprehensive at first, they thought for sure Paula would be stern and commanding, just like Ophelia. But, they were pleasantly surprised with how much kindness she harboured for everyone employed under her care. Working for Paula for two years, they had come to know her genuine nature well.

"One question grandmother, why did you get me to conduct all those tasks?"

The elderly woman sat up tall and sighed. The graceful countenance still lingered on her face, yet there was a certain sadness behind it.

"Now, as you know, the family name and all its inheritance will pass down to a suitable heir when they become of age."

Suddenly the expression on Paula's face changed. These 'matters' her grandmother spoke of were the opposite of what she originally thought. She wasn't in trouble, instead she was getting an advancement of some sort. The young woman knew this day would come; the day she would take over as head of the estate. Paula didn't want to take on this task without her grandmother by her side, but she knew Ophelia would need to depart back to the country and return to her grandfather.

"I know your eighteenth birthday has passed and I should have given this to you earlier but, you now hold the reputation of the Ethel name. You will wear this signet ring with pride and carry out your duties as head of this household."

Ophelia slid the ring off her bony finger and handed it to Paula. The servants were taken aback-they couldn't believe the responsibility was passed on so soon. But, Ophelia was coming on in years and Paula was the only heir left.

Behind the door the two servants began to whisper.

"Did you hear that; Lady Ophelia is going to leave the company to Miss Paula."

"Yes, Clement. I was listening when she said it."

Clement couldn't help but worry a little. He knew Paula was always on her feet, hardly ever taking a break when it came to the welfare of the family. He was apprehensive.

"Surely leaving the tea company to Miss Paula would mean she would have a sudden build-up in pressure?"

Christa scoffed a little.

"Don't worry, Clement. I am sure Lady Ophelia wouldn't give Paula anything she couldn't handle. Besides, we are here to support her."

Christa smiled.

"We'll be here for our mistress no matter what!"

Paula felt teary eyed as she put on her grandmother's ring. She was a little frightened about handling things alone. No doubt she would have a lot more accountability now, but knowing her servants would be at her backing put the lady's mind at ease, especially since they were chosen by her grandmother.

The sun began to set, the twilight reminding Ophelia it was time to return home. The dinner plates were empty, just how Paula's heart felt knowing that her grandmother wouldn't be around to oversee her. Paula and Ophelia made their way outside, the servants following on after. The dusk air was cold, the young lady couldn't help but frown, yet Ophelia only gave the same smile.

"I know you'll do a wonderful job, my dear."

The old woman shared a teary farewell with her granddaughter and entrusted the servants to watch over her. As she lifted one foot onto the carriage step, she turned to say one last thing.

"Paula, I know you're frightened of what happened in the past, but having a butler will ensure your safety. Promise me you'll consider."

The young lady simply nodded.

As the carriage rode out of view, and out of town, a sinking feeling came over the girl. Feeling more relaxed, Christa held onto Paula's arm, reassuring her that all will be all right.

"Mistress, don't look so dreary. We could have some hot chocolate before bed, I'm sure that will lift your spirits."

"That sounds right tasty," Clement drooled.

Paula smiled weakly. The three of them headed back inside, there was still some work to be done before they could retire to bed. Christa needed to tend to the vegetable baskets in the kitchen and Clement had the whole table to clear, not to mention the making of the hot chocolate.

Paula sat down in the living room and fiddled with the ring on her finger. Both her grandparents had a signet ring. Her grandmother's ring was elegant and slim, with a rounded purple jewel, while her grandfather's ring was made with thick gold, holding a smaller square sapphire in the centre. The only similarity in the two pieces of jewellery was the small, golden letters and symbol which were etched into the side. It read 'Ethel' and had an engraving of a rose, highlighting the family crest and surname. Realistically, her grandmother would have passed it down to her mother, and her grandfather would have bestowed it upon her father. But only she stood. If only her mother and father were still here, then she wouldn't need to face these trials alone.

Chapter 3

Fleeting and lost

It was a bitter winter's day, young Paula sat at her desk patiently waiting for the mathematical lecture to end. The only thing she could think of was sitting around the fire with her parents. Before she left for school that morning, the family butler, Jacob, promised a nice cup of tea and ginger biscuits on her return. The memory was burned into her mind. Jacob's emerald eyes were sparkling, his light brown hair swaying in the breeze as he bowed before her. He treated Paula much more like a friend than a noble and the girl preferred it that way.

Charles and Evelyn Ethel waved goodbye on the doorstep that morning. They made sure Paula wore her gloves and scarf as the gales outside began to shrill viciously. Her mother kissed her forehead before she frolicked into the carriage and off to school. Her father reminded her that they had an important meeting and may be late coming home. The little girl didn't mind that, she knew her grandmother would arrive to keep her company.

Back at the manor Charles and Evelyn got dressed for *The Florist's Ball,* a meeting which was held twice a year regarding improvements the nobility would like to implement for their communities. Naturally, Jacob would accompany them. It was just over midday when they departed for the carriage. The chill in the air was numbing, it nipped the skin bright pink and froze the very tips of their noses. Truth be told, the family didn't really want to attend the tedious gathering, but being as wealthy and influential as they were, disregarding an invitation of this degree would stir rumours among the upper classes.

It seemed like years had passed, but the school day was finally over. Just as the girl hypothesised her grandmother, along with the coachman, were there to fetch her. Ophelia and Paula returned home and counted down the hours till the rest of the family would arrive. Paula desperately wanted to show her mother the poem she'd written and play chess with her father, but most of all, she wanted to have a tea party with Jacob. The thought made her warm and smiley, but the girl's innocent daydreams were interrupted when a stern knock came at the door...

Ophelia rushed to open it and was quite baffled when two police officers greeted her. Paula came skipping out of the living room only to be ushered upstairs by her grandmother. She did as she was told, though soundlessly listened atop the stairs. The girl only caught snippets of the conversation, but what she did hear caused tears to stream down her pale cheeks.

She refused to believe it. Her parents... Jacob... they were dead. No, no! They couldn't be, she had waved and kissed them goodbye only that morning. *The officers must have got the wrong house,* she thought as their footsteps faded from earshot. The door clicked shut and her grandmothers' sobs filled the now empty halls. Paula ran down and asked what had happened and after a few shaky breaths, Ophelia explained an incident that the girl couldn't even comprehend in her worst nightmares.

The police had been called to the south side of town, by the stone bridge that ran over the raging river. The carriage, the carriage they were inside, slid off the side of the decaying bridge and plummeted into the raging current below. The officers said her family could have pulled through, yet fate didn't permit them to. The stones from above the bridge broke off, crushing the bodies and leaving them mangled. The officers found four corpses in and around the river. They needed Ophelia to inspect the bodies the next morning and see if she recognised any of them through the damage.

Paula slept in the same bed as her grandmother that night. She refused to stay in her parent's room, she refused to stay alone. None of them slept. Ophelia couldn't process what the officers had described to her and sweet Paula was much too young to understand everything that was unfolding. She just had hope that the officers were wrong and that her parents and Jacob would arrive in the morning. There was no chance they were gone. They couldn't be!

The next day Ophelia went under police protection to identify the bodies. The last thing the officers wanted was another death. They theorised that someone was targeting the Ethel family specifically as their incident was the only known case where more than one member of the family was murdered, thus precautions had to be taken. Ophelia was in utter despair when she confirmed that the bodies were of her son, daughter-in-law, butler, and driver. Their attire and the mark of the family crest were confirmation enough, but the police also handed her a golden rose shaped pin; it was Jacob's pin, signifying he was the Ethel's head butler.

When Ophelia returned, she was pale and trembling. More than that, she came with the same officers as yesterday. Hot tears ran down Paula's face as she realised her family was not coming back. She remembered their goodbyes the day before, and wailed out to the heavens. She thought about her mother's soft cuddles and the way her father ruffled her hair; feelings she will never experience again. As she wept, her grandmother knelt beside her and curled Jacob's pin in her hands. She held it firm, promising to keep it safe forever.

*

The next few years after the tragic incident was a blur. Ophelia and her husband Finley did their best raising Paula in the same London manor their son grew up in. Unsurprisingly, Paula didn't respond well to the drastic change. Sometimes she would wander into her parents' room and squander hours in there, the atmosphere somehow calmed her nerves. She hardly interacted with her grandparents and instead sat on the little plank swing Jacob fashioned for her. Swinging back and forth reminded Paula of how Jacob used to push her so high she imagined she was airborne. The feeling was never the same.

The days went by, and the family spent most of their time indoors. The three couldn't bear to face anyone of the outside world. It was only when Paula turned sixteen that Ophelia felt it was time to hire some servants to stand by her side. Christa was only eighteen when she got the job and Clement, twenty-two Ophelia thought it would be best to hire servants a closer to Paula's age, in that sense the women was right. The two specially selected servants were compassionate but stern. There was no doubt they would support the girl when she took over the estate... that time came all too quickly.

"My lady? You alright?"

A brusque, well accented voice came from behind her. Clement stared at the young woman, worried. The lady stood there, completely immobilised. The chef continued to call out to her until the Paula shook off the hateful recollection.

"Beg your pardon Clement, I was just..." her words trailed off.

"My lady, me and Christa fret over you something silly. We both think you should listen to your grandmother's advice."
The girl's eyes trailed the floor as she stifled a sob.

"I know, I'm sorry."

"I know the past haunts ya, but doing nothing ain't gonna help."

The man's words were the truth. It had been eight years since her family's tragic passing, Paula needed to make a change; her parents would have wanted that. She reached into her pocket and took out a familiar golden pin. The spherical shape taunted her, reminding her that life was nothing more than a cruel replay. Just like a music box, her memories repeated like a faulty tune. She made the decision right there and then: she needed to hire a butler.

*

A few days later, in London's busy town centre, Thomas slumped over a stool at the *Ace of Clubs.* He threw his fist down on the counter-top, demanding another shot of whiskey.

"Another glass!"

"Are you sure, mate? You're looking a bit red in the face," the bartender remarked.

"I said, another glass!" Thomas looked into his eyes.

The bartender was reluctant, but more than happy to oblige when the butler placed a handsome stack of shillings on the countertop. He hastily poured Thomas another glass of whisky. The butler took a couple of gulps then stared at the wall with starry eyes. Even though he was dazed he knew the earlier events well. After the murder of his master he became an unwanted vagabond. The police investigated the case for as long as they could, but with little evidence, they filed it as incomplete and left it to decompose with all the other recent murder cases. One of the uncouth officers even had the audacity to suspect Thomas. A sudden flare of rage came over the butler.

"Damn those stuck-up bastards!" He shook, hauling down the burning alcohol.

Earl Randal was dead. He was the only inheritor to the Randal confectionery company and estate. This meant Thomas was unemployed and friendless. Not to mention his death would come as a shock to the workhouse residents. Without his donations they would be treated unjustly, and most likely die. In the case of a month, Randal's manor and businesses had been sold at auction to the highest bidder.

The ill-mannered family who now possessed ownership of the estate, dismissed Thomas as being incompetent. The head of the family claimed they would not be requiring his services as he looked like a lousy peasant pretending to be part of the gentry! The nobles Thomas once idolised became the people who belittled and tormented him. Perhaps his father was right, perhaps his dream was pathetic all along. Thomas clutched the glass in his hand and grit his teeth, but a sudden recollection of Eric giving his usual small smile levelled his head. He sighed, not all nobles were heartless... just misguided.

In terms of finance, Thomas wasn't sure how he was surviving off the last pay-check he received, but if he kept spending it on alcohol, he would end up a gutter-rat for sure. The public house had become part of his daily routine, it was the only place he could reflect and wallow without anyone criticizing him. He didn't bother telling anyone who he was, or where he came from. If he got too friendly, he reckoned a bunch of reporters would spring out of nowhere to interrogate him on his late master.

And for his current lodgings, it was a cheap inn by a slow running newspaper press. With a belly full of liquor and a splitting headache, Thomas stumbled through the rotting streets of London town and made his way to the foul-smelling inn. '*The Dusty Pillow*', well the name was fitting at least. Never had the butler seen such appalling conditions, but beggars can't be choosers. He faltered into the lobby, shaking his fist at the keeper for calling him a *deadbeat*. As he got to the stairs the shaggy carpet stuck to the sole of his shoes and the cobwebs overhead fell on his tailcoat. He struggled with the key to his room, giving a couple of vagabonds a chance to shove passed him.

"What are you supposed to be? The scruffy haired man snickered.

"Looks like an upper-class wanna be," the skimpy dressed woman spat.

"Why, I say"-

They didn't wait to hear Thomas' comeback, and instead strut past him. The woman mimicked him; "*Why I say*" they both mocked, their snorts echoing all the way down to the lobby. It was hard to believe how vulgar people could be. Thomas never had exposure to such ill treatment at Randal's estate. All he wanted to do was to return home.

As the man finally opened his room door, a hideous space welcomed him. The only furniture present was a tatty bed, an empty cupboard, and a suitcase full of dwindling memories. The atmosphere was sticky; it was probably the remnants of yesterday's distasteful meal that the man refused to touch. Thomas lifted the window (it made a noise similar to a fork scraping against a black-board). The butler inhaled deeply and got a whiff of the autumn roses from St James' park and the aroma of newly drying ink from the press factory in-front.

The wind bellowed, causing some newspapers to fly out of the opposite window, scattering into all directions of the night. One of the papers flew against the piping work beside Thomas' window. He grabbed the loose sheet and held it out in front of him. The headline of the first page read:

'Infamous killer strikes again!'. Baron Arnold Keith had been stabbed in his countryside home, once in the back, twice in the neck... the killer showed no mercy.'

Reading the nightmarish tale made Thomas feel sick, reminding him of the gruesome look Eric pulled when he took his final breath. Six killings in three months... what was happening to the world? Now that the man thought about it, all the killer's victims had one thing in common: they were all nobility.

He remembered the newspaper he read in the cellar that day; the killing occurred in the park. Being in such close proximity to the place of another murder made his nausea surge. If only he remained with Eric that day, then he could have carried out his obligation to the very end...

"Master... why did you depart from me...?"

Thomas' words melted away into the night. He would do anything to get his life back on track. Start from the very beginning, go back to shoe polishing, or even sell his soul to the Devil himself.

Suddenly the breeze blew a calming tune. The wind's sudden change brought composure to the man and he turned the page to continue. The rest of the news was rather cliché; talk of backstreet doctors preforming risky operations, and promiscuous courtesans running amuck in the darkest of places. He was about to head off for another sleepless night when his eye caught the bottom of the page...it was an advertisement for a hiring.

'Now hiring experienced butler for Ethel manor in the outskirts of London. Skills needed: cleaning, cooking, task management, and advanced English speaking. For more details file queries by letter, and post to Miss Paula Ethel of the Ethel estate.'

The butler couldn't believe his luck! It was as if the role was made for him! He took a quill and some parchment and scribbled down his details. He also enquired about the number of hours he would need to preform, and the sum of money he would obtain. For the first time in a long time, he didn't feel so lost.

Chapter 4

Fateful encounter

The post had arrived right on schedule. Paula had received a newspaper and a postcard from her grandfather, as well as a few odd letters regarding her advertisement. She sat near the greenhouse, savouring the scent of fresh flowers and the autumn sun. If she were lucky, the change of atmosphere may have a good effect on her mood.

"How's the hunt going, my lady?"

Christa watered the rosemary and mint baskets clutching onto the greenhouse door, looking back at Paula who was sipping on a cup of English Breakfast.

"It could be better, Christa. I fear no decent applicant will answer my writings," she exhaled.

None of the responses she looked over were fitting. Some of the candidates were not suitably experienced, while others were much too elderly to keep up with the fast-paced responsibilities expected of an Ethel family butler. The lady sighed and plucked up another letter.

"This won't do, I'm afraid I will never find another butler quite like... Jacob..."

Paula uttered the latter of that sentence quietly, not wanting Christa to catch wind of what she said and start coddling her.

Getting to the bottom of the pile, she halted at a form written in dainty blue-ink. She began to read, her features lifting as she scanned every word.

"Could it be...?"

Christa looked up and hurried to the chair Paula was reclined in. When reading the applicant's name, a glimpse of familiarity flickered on her face.

"Thomas Fulton...? I could swear I've heard that name before."

Christa scratched her chin as she read the name again. Paula kept reading and was keen to see the applicant had past experiences too.

"His skills will make him perfect for this role," Paula smiled.

The lady took some ink and a quill and began to promptly write a response. She had agreed to arrange a meeting with the butler to discuss the working hours and living arrangements. If all went well, Mr Fulton would be the new addition to the Ethel household.

*

Back at the inn, Thomas was surprised to see a letter sent to the inn keeper's desk. It was listed as high priority and was hand-delivered by another servant that very same day. The tiny, curly script was incredibly neat and well-written, even the signature on the bottom line was sheer perfection.

'Dear Mr Thomas Fulton,

Thank you for your swift response on my commercial. I'm pleased to inform you that you are eligible for a meeting with me in my estate. We will discuss your past experiences, the workload and responsibilities, as well as a little bit about the Ethel estate and history. Please come by at one o'clock in the afternoon.

Yours sincerely,

Paula Ethel'

The man couldn't believe it! He actually received a response! He held the letter out in front of him and took-in a long breath.

"There's no point waiting about here..." he whispered to himself.

Thomas brushed his dark brunet hair till it was free of tangles, cleaned all the dust and lint from his tailcoat, and slipped on his cotton gloves. The man felt renewed, like the first day he put on a butler's uniform.

Thomas left the *Dusty Pillow* feeling confident. As soon as he stepped outside, the sun lit up his green eyes. He walked past the markets and houses, following the directions written on the other side of the letter.

"Hmm, just at the edge of town I see..."

The butler reached the foothills of unspoilt land. Just from observing his surroundings, he knew he was getting closer to private property.

"I better hail a carriage for the rest of the way...or perhaps an omnibus..." he mused.

*

In the afternoon an enthusiastic knock came at the door. Paula was startled, she wasn't expecting anyone to arrive so soon. Thomas was surprised when who he assumed to be the lady of the manor welcomed him instead of a servant. Although he wasn't complaining.

47

The young lady was extremely beautiful, with her black braided hair, and doll-like features. He smiled widely and held out the letter.

"Are you... Miss Paula?"

"Indeed I am. You must be Mr Fulton, correct?"

"Yes, apologies if I arrived a bit early."

"Not at all. Your initiative is most appreciated," the Lady gestured for him to come inside.

Thomas felt even more privileged when hearing her melodious voice. He made up his mind; he was going to do everything in his power to impress Miss Paula. They both took a seat in the living room and began discussing business. Paula felt the man possessed most rudimentary skills and seemed well organised, however, when it came to talk about where he previously worked, the lady's face fell.

"You were Earl Randal's butler?" The man nodded. Even though the event had taken place over a month ago, Thomas' desperate attempts to overcome his trauma were unsuccessful. This was the part of the interrogation he wanted to avoid. What would the lady think now that she knew he failed to protect his last master? But instead of prying on the man's previous life, the young woman asked him if he was all right. Thomas was not expecting that; in all the time he spent grieving, no one cared to ask him how he felt.

"My parents knew Richard Randal, Eric's father. All of them provided donations to the workhouse, some of the very few noble families who did."

The butler looked up. In all his years of service Eric never mentioned word of his family, yet the Ethel's were once acquainted with them. Paula continued to comfort Thomas, assuring him the incident was not his fault. The man felt relieved to finally talk with someone. The door to the living room swung open. The other two servants entered with a tray of tea and finger sandwiches. Paula had a feeling they were being exceptionally hospitable to get a glimpse of Mr Fulton. She smiled to herself as Clement and Christa introduced themselves to the man.

"It's right nice to meet you mate! I'm Clement Morris, the head chef around here," Clement grasped Thomas' hand in a firm shake.

"And my name is Christa Wood, I'm Miss Paula's gardener. It's very nice to have you with us," Christa curtsied, and smiled gracefully.

Thomas was over the moon to know that he wouldn't be the only servant in the manor. He grinned at them both, laying a hand on his chest as he bowed.

"It's a pleasure to meet the both of you. I do hope I'll see you again."

Clement put his hands in his pockets and swung back and forth on his heels. Mr Fulton seemed decent enough, but was he tailored to be an Ethel servant? Clement wasn't so sure but decided to be pleasant all the same.

"I'm sure you'll get the job, then us three will be the best of mates,"

Clement let out a chuckle before departing with Christa who also wondered if the man could adjust to the standards Mrs Ophelia had implemented in the manor long before him.

"My, my, I haven't seen those two so energetic before. Your presence really is a blessing Mr Fulton."

The man felt like he was blushing, he had never been called a blessing by anyone.

"Why thank you, Miss Paula."

The two talked further, discussing Thomas' former job as well as his childhood dreams.

Soon it was Paula's turn to enlighten him on her past. She would rather not, but it was only fair that Thomas knew the truth if he was going to work for her. She informed him about the horrid incident and about how her family was cruelly taken from her. At the end of the tale Thomas couldn't begin to comprehend the agony Paula must have gone through. He only just discovered grief himself, but the young woman before him must have been grieving for many years.

"I'm so sorry, Miss Paula."

The lady mustered a faux smile and thanked Thomas for his understanding. Intrusive thoughts in the back of her head told her the man would turn and leave now that he knew of these prior events, but he just looked at her. After some hesitation, Paula spoke her mind.

"I understand if you no longer want to consider working here."

Thomas was stunned at her words. It's not as if the man would pass a grand opportunity like this one. After all, it wasn't Miss Paula who committed such a horrendous deed. Fate is unkind, he knew that. He didn't blame the lady for what happened and learning the truth just made him more determined to help her.

"In all seriousness Miss Paula, I would be honoured to get the job."

The girl almost dropped her teacup. This man was either hopelessly desperate, or honestly sincere... maybe he was a bit of both or perhaps he had an ulterior motive of some kind. Ulterior motive or not, the man did fit her requirements and clearly demonstrated his passion for being a butler. There was no visible reason to refuse him.

"Very well Mr Fulton, you've got the job."

"Thank you, my lady,"

Thomas stood and shook Paula's hand. As the two of them exited the living room the other two servants leaped back from the door with guilty looks on their faces. The excitement was so unbearable they couldn't stop themselves from eavesdropping. Thomas grasped their hands confidently.

"I will see you all tomorrow." Clement and Christa looked at one another-holding-in their excitement.

The man waved goodbye at the door and left with a smooth bow. His eyes never left Paula's as he walked down the road. Once the carriage had reached town again, Thomas returned to the *Dusty Pillow* with more charisma than ever. He ignored all the other misfits around him, walking smugly past the keeper too. He got to his room and began to pack his luggage as quickly as he could, thankful he would never have to set foot in such a cretinous place again.

From tomorrow, no one would dare call him a vagabond, for he would be serving the esteemed Ethel manor.

Chapter 5

Her butler

As expected, Thomas returned to the Ethel manor at 7 o'clock sharp. He was attired in a crisp black suit, a slim tie and white gloves. Carrying nothing but a suitcase in hand, he knocked on the door keenly awaiting to see Miss Paula. The lady's eyes widened as she observed the man on the doorstep. Despite yesterday's discussion, Paula still had a little voice of doubt telling her the wandering butler would never return to her humdrum life, but... he delivered. Paula welcomed the man inside with a hearty grin.

"Welcome back, Mr Fulton," she gestured for him to enter.

"I am overjoyed to be here," Thomas said.

"We are overjoyed to have you with us," she escorted him through the front room and up the stairs to his new quarters, "Things will be orderly with you here, I'm sure."

He smiled. His room was close to the landing, just a hall away from Paula's chambers.

"Please take all the time you need to settle, and come to the living room once you've finished."

"Wait mistress..."

The lady stopped in the doorway, giving the man a thoughtful look.

"Where are all the other servant's quartered?" the butler asked.

"Oh, Clement and Christa are on the ground floor, closer to the kitchen and pantries."

The butler wasn't sure what to think. He always believed the servants of a manor slept in one room[2], but maybe he was mistaken.

Paula inspected the man's puzzled features. Could this arrangement be awkward for him?

"I hope this room doesn't inconvenience you."

The butler waved his hands dismissively, his pupils broadening.

"Oh no, not at all. I was just curious, my lady."

"Very well. See you in a moment then," Paula slipped back in the hallway.

---

[2] Female servants usually quartered in the attic while male servants quartered on the ground floor; however Paula's manor is an exception as there are only four servants, one not even living in the manor.

Thomas took a deep breath and turned the doorknob to his new quarters. He had a brown and white themed room with a single-bed in the centre. A chest of draws and a large oak wardrobe also stood against the wall. There was a supplementary cream rug on the side of the bed, as well a windowsill sitting area. This would be his chambers from here on out, a much better arrangement than that infernal inn. After placing his additional clothes and shoes in the wardrobe, the butler strolled downstairs to where Paula was writing in the living room.

"Ah Fulton, here's the list of duties you will perform daily. Of course, additional tasks will come up from time to time."
Thomas skimmed the list of chores. There were various tasks ranging from cooking to dusting, piano practise with the mistress and helping with the meal service.

"We'll see how you adjust. After you have mastered these tasks, your duties will begin to revolve around my needs."
The butler nodded, remembering how Eric requested he learn the violin so he could conduct lessons with him. At some point Thomas even taught him to properly knot his bow ties. Getting to know his master was the

best part of becoming a butler and he was looking forward to getting to know Paula too.

"One more thing..." she added, with a slight smile.

Paula inched closer to the man and placed Jacob's gold, rose-shaped pin on his tailcoat. Thomas looked down as the girl locked the pin onto his collars and noticed she had a message written on the front of her wrist.

"This pin indicates you are now the Ethel's head butler, wear it with pride."

"I will. Thank you, my lady."
Paula left with a half-smile. Passing on Jacob's pin was a challenging step, but a necessary one. The more she forced herself to move forward the further old memories could drown. As the lady left Thomas to his own devices, he briefly thought about the writing on her wrist. The man could not dwell on his questions for long however, as he heard clamouring coming from the kitchen.

The first task of the day: prepare breakfast. Thomas made his way to the kitchen; he was grateful that Christa was nearby to point him in the right direction or he may not have found it at all. He stepped inside the immaculate room, where Clement was already plating some crumpets. The chef beamed when he saw the butler.

"You doing alright, mate? First day on the job, ya must be thrilled!"

"Yes indeed, I'm ready to start the day." Thomas said, taken aback by the open friendliness.

Clement let out a chuckle as he flipped some berries in a saucer.

"Start? I've already finished making breakfast for the mistress."

Thomas looked a little deflated.

"O-oh, I see."

"Don't fret mate, us lot still need to eat something. I'll tell you a trick. If you want to cook for the mistress, try asking her what she wants for breakfast the night before or early the next morning. She'll be right happy if you come to wake her."

The chef smirked cheekily and ran out of the kitchen with a plate of crumpets, fresh cream and sautéed berries.

Waking up the mistress? Well it was a true fact; a butler must get up before anyone else and starts his day by waking up his master. Nonetheless, he never did such things for Eric. Come to think of it, Thomas had never entered Eric's chambers before. While aimlessly thinking of his late master, the butler's mind reverted to his new mistress-it seems like she was hiding something too. What could she have written on her wrist which was so important she couldn't fetch a piece of parchment for? The butler considered for a couple of minutes, only to be interrupted by Clement.

"Come on mate! We still got work to be getting on with!"

"Of course, sorry about that."

The chef began frying some sausages and toasted some bread. He glanced Thomas' way and noticed his mind wasn't completely immersed in cooking.

"What's on your mind, mate?" Clement's question caught the man off guard, he wasn't used to getting chummy with people, especially since being outcast. But since the chef seemed remotely concerned about him, Thomas replied.

"Well you see, the mistress had some writing on her wrist. I was just wondering about that..."

The brawny brunet looked intrigued. He put down the pan he was scouring and faced the butler.

"Well, what did it say?"

Thomas recalled the brief encounter with Paula and tried to envision the inky message etched on her skin.

"I believe it said, '*only a white rose*'."

Thomas hadn't the faintest clue what the message meant, but just as he was going to wave the conversation off Clement threw his palms on the table. His eyes burned with resolve and his mouth revealed a pearly smile.

"Come on mate? Don't you know the meaning of a while rose?"

Thomas shook his head. Clement let out an exaggerated sigh and brought a hand to his head.

"It's simple really. Giving someone a white rose means your love for them is the truest of true, the purest of pure."

The butler only stopped and stared. He was no expert in romance, but he always believed a red rose was used as an affectionate gesture.

"Are you sure you don't mean a red rose, Clement?"

"No mate, a red rose is cliché, common, completely expected. Giving someone a red rose is like saying 'Ello, you're ordinary, here's an unoriginal gift to express my love'."

Thomas gave it some deeper thought, and surprisingly, the chef had a valid point.

"A white rose, eh? I'll remember that one."
Clement chuckled and turned back to the stove. They still had the task of fixing-up breakfast for themselves.

"Anyway, I think I fancy tomatoes, egg, and toast today." Clement said.
Tomatoes, egg, and toast? That's something the butler could easily do. Thomas took some eggs from a little woven basket and cracked them over the pan. Scrambled eggs and beans will go nicely with Clement's toast.

"I'm glad you're here mate, the work will get done twice as quickly."

"I'm glad to be here. I never thought I'd get to work alongside others."
Clement went unusually quiet. His voice no longer sounded cheerful and energetic but more sympathetic.

"You must have had it rough mate, but let's hope things will be dandy from here on out. Yeah?"

The two of them continued to prepare breakfast. Soon enough there were three steaming plates of fluffy egg, toast, poached tomato and sweet beans. Christa moseyed into the kitchen, looking as hungry as a horse.

"I'm starved! What have we got for today?"

The two men whirled around, holding knives and forks in their hands. Clement rubbed the back of his neck and beheld the gardener.

"We're in luck today Christa! Thanks to Mr Fulton's hard work we've got a whole load of breakfast to tuck into!"

Christa folded her arms, and gave a small pout.

"You were going to eat without me, weren't you?"

A bead of sweat formed on the chef's forehead as he avoided eye contact.

"Uhm... no?" Clement said.

Unexpectedly, Christa leaped at Clement and pulled him by his ear. She started yelling at him, all while the chef tried to run from her clutches. Thomas sat himself at the kitchen table and watched the other two servants in amusement. He was indulging in his breakfast, so only caught bits of Christa's shouting. It went something like, *"you always do this Morris"*, *"it's not fair, we need to share the food!"* The rest of the lecture was incoherent, but the yelps and pleas from Clement were all too clear.

*

It was fortunate Christa accepted Clement's apology, finally the three of them could resume eating their delectable meal. Thomas didn't realise how little time he had to eat, not until the other two servants stood up abruptly with spotless plates.

"Right, let's get back to it!" the gardener hummed happily.

"Right you are, Christa!"
Clement got up and rubbed his stomach. He looked at Thomas, who just finished the last of his toast. Giving a hearty smile, he patted his back light-heartedly.

"Well that was right nice. We'll see you later at lunch, mate," Clement winked. Christa bowed and excused herself, she had the heavy chore of pulling out the weeds and trimming all the front hedges. Clement took the dishes to the sink and whistled a wistful tune as he started washing. Thomas took out the list Paula gave him earlier; the next task was to dust the living room.

When the butler entered the room, the duster was already resting against the wall. He didn't pay it much mind and instead listened to the fire crackling lowly. Even though the other servants were only a few rooms away, the deafening silence reminded the butler of the days he spent unaccompanied in Randal's manor. Despite the unsavoury memories skimming his mind, Thomas continued to dust the trinkets on the mantelpiece. There was a lovely picture sitting in front of him; it was of young Paula and who he assumed to be the rest of the Ethel family. There was a man who was a spitting image of the girl; no doubt that was her father. Next to him was Paula's mother and behind her was Lady Ophelia, he guessed. A short elderly man crouched beside Paula's grandmother; that was probably Finley Ethel. On the far left of the photo stood a young woman with brunette hair and brown eyes. She had a pitiful expression on her face and was quite a distance from the rest of the family.

"Fulton, it's time for my piano lesson."
Paula skipped into the room to see her butler observing the family photo. Thomas turned around, looking like he was bottling a burning question.

"Mistress, who is this?"
Paula walked up to the picture frame and studied where Thomas was pointing.

"Oh, that's..."

Her tone went dramatically sombre. Thomas didn't understand, had he overstepped?

"That's my aunt Cordelia. I only ever saw her on occasion, then she disappeared." The butler preferred not to pry, but since he was working for the Ethel family now he concluded it wouldn't hurt to ask.

"What happened to her?"
The man was expecting a long tragedy, but what he really got was strange to say the least.

"I wish I knew. Anytime I asked grandmother or grandfather they just ignored me as if I hadn't said anything at all." Thomas looked perplexed. It wasn't as if Paula was enquiring about a stranger. It made the man wonder what Ophelia was hiding...

"Anyway, shall we start my music lesson?"
Paula ambled towards the door. With one final glance at the photograph, Thomas followed her to the parlour.

The young woman was eager to be seated behind the grand piano, she gently tickled the keys in front of her. Just for an instant, Thomas observed the lady's pureness and smiled to himself.

"Let's see here."

The man reached out and took the sheet music from the stand. His brows elevated when he read the name of the melody, '*Gymnopedie*'. This particular piece was becoming quite popular, it was composed by Erik Satie, a young and unconventional musician who took blessed listeners on a journey of equanimity and emotional discovery[3]. Thomas did admit he was quite the connoisseur when it came to classical music.

"This is a very soothing piece; I would be honoured to hear you play."
Thomas stood tall and listened intently as Paula brushed the first notes. She played the introduction very well, but as she got midway, she fumbled with the keys and tripped over the tune. The girl paused brusquely, eyeing the notes in front of her.

"It's no good, I can't get this bit right."
The man took a seat next to her and angled his fingers above the piano. His instinct took over a little. He was, after all, used to giving lessons in music.

---

[3] It is recommended to listen to the classical piece, *Gymnopedie by Erik Satie* to fully immerse yourself in this scene.

"It looks to me as if you haven't grasped using two hands yet. Start from the top, once more."

The lady swallowed and played the first notes as good as she did before. Thomas followed midway and played the low keys.

"You see mistress, all you need is some guidance."

The two of them played in perfect sync. Paula delicately skimmed the high keys and Thomas easily hit the lows. The serene melody filled their ears and hearts. It was oddly nostalgic for the both of them; Paula had first heard this piece from one of her father's piano lessons and Thomas was fortunate enough to experience this music at the opera, though it was a long time ago.

The lady looked over at Thomas. He appeared carefree as he swayed to the rhythm of the music. The lady bit her lip and realised something... Jacob was the family butler, but Thomas was all hers.

Chapter 6

Masquerade

Paula awoke the next morning to a faint knocking at her door. She tossed and turned amongst the thick covers until the feeling of drowning in cushions felt worse than having to get up.

"May I come in, mistress?"
When hearing Thomas' voice Paula bolted upright; she fiddled with the curly fringe covering her eyes and watched the door prudently.

"You may enter."

The lady tried to put on her best voice despite being sleep deprived and a little embarrassed. On some rare occasions she was awoken by Clement and Christa. She was even awoken once in the middle of the night when the sweet gardener thought she saw a ghost, (of course, it wasn't a ghost and instead a barn owl) but even so, being greeted by Thomas first thing in the morning... it felt different and for some reason, made her stomach all tingly.

"Good morning, my lady."

Thomas entered with a tray of Ceylon tea and Marie biscuits[4]. The man plucked the wax covered candelabra off the night-stand and replaced it with the tray of sweet morsels. The lady gazed up at him while he took what was left of the candles out of the holders.

"How did you know I like sweet things?"

"Clement may have told me," he smiled.

The lady took a biscuit and bit into it cheerfully. After finishing the biscuit, she loomed over the cup of Ceylon tea. Having her own tea shop meant she was good at criticising flavours but out of all the brews she sampled, her favourite was by far earl grey.

"What would you like for breakfast today, my lady?"

"Umm, maybe a mushroom omelette with buttered bread and golden syrup."

Thomas wasn't sure if it was just his ears or did Paula sound extraordinarily adorable when she was thinking aloud? He shook his head, looking over his shoulder.

---

[4] Marie biscuits were invented in the 1870s. Its modern equivalent is the Rich Tea biscuit.

"I'll prepare breakfast for you right away, mistress. Come down whenever you're ready."

With one last bow, he left the room and went downstairs. Paula placed her teacup on the saucer with a clunk. She closed her eyes and thought about the day before. Playing the piano in a duet was so thrilling! The lady had a feeling her days would never again be dull with Thomas around.

"Good mornin' mistress!"
As soon as she stepped into the dining room, a very lively Clement was there to greet her.

"Good morning Clement, how are the chores getting along?"
Clement rushed over to the lady with fiery eyes.

"Well my lady, you'll never guess what... Mr Fulton has already finished most of the morning chores!"

"My goodness, already?" Said Paula. Thomas was adapting to his duties as head butler smoothly, however Paula hadn't expected anything less.

"Who'd have thought he could have done so well within a day. He must have picked up some dandy skills from working for Mr Randal!"

Clement paused mid-conversation, remembering he had to set the table. Paula sat down in her favourite armchair, briefly thinking about her old friend Eric, and how she wished she had seen him one last time.

The girl found herself getting lost in the vase of exotic flowers in front of her. Every now and again Christa would cut the extra flowers from the garden and display them around the manor, but the gorgeous florae staring back at her looked extraordinarily beautiful today.

"You like the flowers, my lady?"

Thomas appeared from behind her and placed a hot plate of omelette, mushroom and sweet, buttery bread. Everything from the colour to the presentation of the food looked exactly like how the girl envisioned it in her head. Turning away from her breakfast, the lady nodded.

"Oh yes, these flowers are simply exquisite. By any chance... were you the one who picked them?"

Thomas was amazed, how did Paula know that? Did the flowers really look that out of place?

"Why yes, my lady, I did."

Paula could not tear her eyes away from the bold purple blossoms.

"You must pick some more when they wither," Paula whispered.

The lady reminisced in the flower's prettiness while eating her breakfast, which was one of the best meals she had ever eaten.

*

The morning went as promptly as the last and before Paula knew it she had some free time on her hands.

"My lady! A letter arrived!"
Christa came leaping out of the front garden, holding a wax-stamped letter in her hand.

"Hmm... a letter for me?"

Paula flipped the letter over before cutting the envelope with an extravagant letter opener. It was sent from *Lady Audrey Young*. Paula almost let her emotions get the better of her. That name. After all these years, Audrey still remembered her.

Audrey was one of Paula's greatest and most trustworthy childhood friends. They spent a fair amount of time with each other at school, but after the death of Paula's parents their time together was cut short.

"What does it say, my lady?"

Christa broke the lady's daydream and gazed at her with curious eyes.

"It's an invitation to a masquerade ball, from lady Young."

Out of nowhere, Clement appeared beside Paula.

"Yeah, I remember Mrs Ophelia talkin' about her when we were first brought in."

"That's right, she did," Christa nodded in agreement.

"Well yes, as you know Lady Young was a good friend of mine."

The girl wondered what Audrey must look like now, back when they were youngsters, she had straightened ginger hair and bold brown eyes. She never wore fancy clothing like the rest of the girls, and instead favoured plain, simple dresses. Some part of Paula told her to embrace change, years of no contact... what where the chances Audrey would be the same bubbly girl.

"I'm entrusting the manor to you three when I go," said Paula.

Paula turned to leave but Thomas stepped in front of her.

"With all due respect, mistress, I think I should accompany you to this ball."

The other two servants glanced at each other with straight faces. They couldn't determine which option was better-having Thomas stay at the manor would mean they could finish the chores twice as quickly, but the mistress being safe was far more important.

"With the increase in crime... it will be safer for you if I came along," Thomas stated coolly.

Paula gave up the argument quicker than the servants thought. She was going to object at first, but thinking back to the gruesome headlines in the paper; it was enough to make her accept Thomas' offer.

"Aright Fulton, you can join me."

Without another word the lady strolled up the stairs and out of sight. The butler turned to the other servants and redirected them to their daily chores. Clement went back to cleaning the kitchen and Christa ornamented the downstairs corridor with silver candelabras.

*

Paula leaned her head close to the golden mirror at her bedside. Something bubbled inside her stomach, a feeling she hadn't experienced in a long time: disbelief. She couldn't shake off the revelations brewing in her mind. It was odd, getting an invitation to a ball out of the blue, especially from someone she had not spoken to in years. The lady exhaled hot breath on the mirror, causing her reflection to blur and twist. She clutched the envelope in her hand, occasionally referring to the clock. The Ethel's had always taken pride in their reputation. It would stir quite the uproar if she did not attend an honoured party like this one. All at once she gathered her uncertainties and stood. Disappointing her family was something she couldn't bear. The thought occurred to her quite late, but she didn't even have an outfit to wear to this ball.

"Mistress..."

There was a soft knock at the door.

"I brought you something to wear for the ball, mistress."

Thomas entered holding a bundle of grey clothing in hand. He unravelled the outfit on the bed. It was an elegant grey dress with slightly puffed cream sleeves, a low frilly lace bordered the collarbone. It had strings athwart the back to tighten it and a silky cream ribbon around the waist. Thomas handed her something else-it was a beaked mask with graceful white and black feathers emerging out the top.

"Oh... it's absolutely beautiful."

"I'm glad you like it, my lady."

They smiled at each other for a few moments, until Thomas spoke again,

"A simple matter such as finding a dress, you do not have to worry about small details like that now."

Before the girl could reply, the man bowed and left the room. Paula let her eyes observe the last few movements of the door handle before looking over the ensemble again. How did Thomas know what she was worried about...? She shook her head dismissively. It didn't matter. Now she had no excuse to avoid the upcoming soirée.

It was for the best she attended; she thought while exiting her room. The ball was in a week, this gave the girl plenty of time to finish her reading and independent writing sessions.

"I reckon I have sufficient time to continue my reading..."

Paula sang those words as she treaded down the hall. The lady pushed aside a wide double door. As soon as it opened the scent of fresh pages and ink tickled her nose. Paula was grateful to have such a grand library. She trailed her hand over the spines of a few books, it was Jacob's influence that got her immersed into reading and now she found she could not stay away. Recently, she had finished *Alice in wonderland*. She found the book to be quite refreshing with the odd mix of characters and dream-like plot, the white rabbit was by far her favourite character. The young woman got a little vexed when she came across a shelf of books that were ordered incorrectly. She scanned each spine: there was *Romeo and Juliet, A Study in Scarlet,* and a strange black leather book[5]. Shaking her head, she slid out Romeo and Juliet and carried it tightly under her arm.

When she arrived downstairs Clement was buffing the silver cutlery at the dining table. Paula sat down in the chair next to him, giving him a friendly smile. The man was instantly intrigued by her new book. He adored enquiring about his mistress's stories, fascinated by the diverse characters and twisted endings.

"Reading a new book, I see mistress."

"Oh yes, I find Shakespeare's works to be a particularly good read."

Clement didn't mind what book Paula discussed with him, he just liked to gain as

---

[5] Readers who have come across my first novella will be familiar with this peculiar leather book.

much knowledge as he could. He couldn't help it, when he was a young boy his parents never let him have a real education. He never went to school and he never learned how to read properly. He got told the basics: handwriting, spelling and low-level grammar but he never learned about classic pieces of literature, poetry, or famous books. He hoped one day he could read all the greats and gain a sense of accomplishment. There was however one thing his parents taught him, the value of hard work and manual labour. It must have been his sheer determination and hands-on experience which got him this job. If it weren't for that, he wasn't sure where he'd be now.

"So, mistress, how did that last book of yours end...?"

The two must have been talking for at least a few hours, Paula was more than happy to comprehend all the aspects in Alice in wonderland, and Clement intently listened to every word.

*

The next few days went by like lightning. Paula read with Clement every day, getting to study and help Clement read was far more fulfilling then reading on her own. When she ended her discussion on *Great Expectations* with the chef, Thomas emerged from the garden. Bits of yellowing leaves covered his shoes, it impressed Paula he was able to do the garden work so quickly.

"My lady, it is almost time to depart for the ball."

Paula eyed the clock hanging above the mantle place. Thomas didn't jest! Time had really snuck-up on them.

"Beg your pardon Fulton, Clement." The girl gave a hasty curtsey before darting upstairs to her quarters.

Once entering her room, Paula slipped her dress over her corset, struggling with the ribbons and her best shoes. After staring in the mirror she put on the crow's mask and stroked the upturned feathers.

"My lady? Are you alright in there?"

"Yes, I'm fine," she stuttered.

The butler entered non-the-less, clearly disregarding Paula's rapid response. As if by magic Thomas' shoes were spotless. The leaves that once smothered them had vanished, no one would have guessed he was raking leaves just a few moments before.

"Erm, are you ready to go Fulton?" Paula turned to leave, but froze when a warm breath caressed her neck.

"Honestly, mistress. These strings are all tangled..."

Thomas pulled on the strings and lace at the back of her dress, occasionally his fingers brushed against the bare nape of her neck. She shivered under the faint traces. Thomas was only tightening her dress but it felt... oddly sensual...

"There you go, mistress; we can head off now."

"Umm... right you are Fulton, let's be on our way."

After giving brief instructions to the other two servants, and layering up in long coats, the two went off to Lady Audrey's ball.

The coach ride was mostly silent, although sometimes the butler and lady engaged in some small talk. At other times, Paula would let herself travel along with the rolling scenery. She had her eyes peeled, scouting out the antiquated manor sleeping under the green cliff-side.

"We've arrived Miss Paula," Cliffe, the coachman, called out from the outer-seat.

Thomas unlocked the door and took his lady's hand, helping her down the carriage steps. As they walked side-by-side one of the horses nudged Paula's back. It neighed in distress, dragging its hooves across the unsettled ground.

"Sorry aboot that, Miss. Ah'll settle the horses doon and wait for your return," he said.

Cliffe dropped the reins and hopped out of the driver's seat. He tipped his hat in apology and patted the horses' snout. That was certainly odd, the horses were normally so well behaved, and never usually did anything out of protocol. Looking back with furrowed brows, Thomas and Paula continued to walk through the golden gated entrance and off towards the slumbering manor. The austere looking maid at the door inspected Paula's invitation, then bowed slowly.

"Good evening Lady Ethel, we are delighted you could join us today. Please do come in."

The maid welcomed the guests with an inquisitive simper. Paula didn't recall Audrey ever talking about a maid in their youth, she must have been hired one quite recently. As soon as Paula steeped inside the ballroom, a ginger haired woman in a peacock mask danced over and hugged her without taking a breath.

"Aww Paula! I've missed you dearly!"

"Audrey....?"

The women stood back and tilted her head. Paula was quite staggered that Audrey recognised her even when she was wearing a mask. Maybe it's true what sceptics say: The eyes are a window to the soul.

"Well of course you ninny, you haven't forgotten about me, have you?" Audrey winked playfully with a smile.

"No, not at all. I remember the times we had, and I wanted to come back but..."

Paula frowned as the thought of her parents crossed her mind. Audrey saw the flicker of sorrow and wagged her finger dismissively.

"No, no, no, Paula, I won't have you upsetting yourself. You are here to enjoy yourself!"

Paula gave a soft smile and nodded. Audrey really hadn't changed. As if noticing Thomas for the first time Audrey twirled around him and lifted a hand to her chin.

"Hmm, you're a fetching one, aren't you? I don't believe I've had the pleasure of making your acquaintance."

Thomas bowed, his seamless features glinting in the mellow lighting overhead.

"My name's Thomas Fulton, Miss Paula's newly hired butler. It's a delight to meet you Miss Young."

Audrey's cheeks drained to pink.

"Ooh, Paula! You got yourself such a looker..."

"Audrey!"

The two woman were acting as if they were back in school, giggling shyly over strapping boys in uniform who'd daily walk past the building's exterior. Thomas stood in between them, flustered and red faced. From the right he was being teased by Miss Young and from the left he was being tormented by his mistresses' loveable conduct. The man couldn't decide if he wanted them to stop or continue.

Reverting back to a collective state, the two women spent some time chatting with each other. Paula learned Audrey was also taking more responsibilities in her estate and was enjoying her time with her maid, Agatha Turner. Audrey knew about the Ethel family's gruesome incident, but hearing the events in person were far more horrific than reading about them in the paper.

"I'm so sorry, Paula."

"Don't fret, Audrey. I'm managing a lot better now."

Thomas stepped forward and stood by his mistress. All the support was helping Paula with her anxieties, and meeting a friend from her childhood brought back fond memories. At the end of it all, Paula was glad she came along to the ball.

Chapter 7

Narrow escape

With all the merry making Paula needed to take a rest, she sat on a table at the far-side of the room and stretched her legs. Removing her mask, she observed the masses of nobles dancing and drinking. The lady drifted far off into memory lane as she observed all the passing faces, even managing to recognise some of the guests bustling about the place.

A tall, dark haired women was boasting about her fur scarf at the banquet table, Paula remembered her to be Duchess Nora Price. The girl met her once when she was younger, at one of the famed Ethel garden parties if she were correct. Looking over to the right, the girl saw an old, scrawny man swigging shots of bourbon whiskey. Ah, that had to be the Viscount Landers. He reminded Paula of her grandfather, minus all the heavy drinking. Looking across the hall to where most were waltzing, the young woman observed a slim young man gazing at the orchestra. He possessed white-blond hair and light-grey eyes, his childish captivation for the violin brought a smile to Paula's lips. With some intricate thinking, she realised he was Earl Archie. She couldn't quite put her finger on his last name, but knew her parents had them acquainted when they were toddlers.

There were also foreign royalty and esteemed diplomats sitting on the upper balcony. An Indian princess... a Chinese businessman and, someone else? Paula could only catch a glimpse from where she was sitting but hoped one day she could make enough progress in her tea company to one day trade with gentleman and woman like that. The girl daydreamed and turned her attention to the window. Audrey's innovatively sculpted garden was in full-bloom. When beholding the large hedge maze surrounded by bluebells and hyacinths the girl gasped. The walls must have been at least four metres high! Now that she recalled, Audrey was obsessed with puzzles and mazes when they were younger, often creating confusing obstacles in the school hall for them to conquer.

"Mistress?"

Thomas bowed and took a seat beside Paula.

"Oh, hello Fulton."

"What's the matter, my lady? Why are you sitting so far away?"

Paula rested her chin in her hands and gazed into the man's bright green eyes.

"Let's just say I'm still getting used to venturing outside. It's still a little daunting for me."

The butler shuffled his chair closer to the lady, then fell into a whisper.

"My lady, I promise to chase your anxieties away," whispered Thomas.

Paula rested her hands back on the table, her eyes thoughtful.

The man caught a lump in his throat... "No matter where you are I'll... what I mean is, you have my support, my lady."

Suddenly Audrey came sprinting out of the bubbling crowd, arms linked with a slender, older looking man.

"Paula, I need to introduce you to someone!" Audrey said.

The man Audrey was clinging onto was wearing a black sequinned mask which oddly resembled that of a plague doctor's guise. The gentleman had narrow hazel eyes and slicked caramel-brown hair. His skin was a golden sunset and his voice had foreign notes to them... perhaps even tropical.

"Good evening, Lady Ethel."

The man took the lady's hand and kissed the back of it, he let his hazel pupils meet Paula's blue pools for just an instant.

"Paula, this is Duke Alister Knox... a man very close to my heart."

Audrey giggled under her breath. She always got giddy around handsome men, but this time her behaviour was much sillier and uncontrollable. Alister coiled a lock of Audrey's hair behind her ear, the young lady blushed in response. Paula was not sure what to feel, a part of her was pleased for her friend but the other part was devastated... and a tad jealous. How was it fair that Audrey had her family, her friends and a lover, while Paula had most of that taken away from her? Scowling for just a second, Paula unclenched her first and mustered her best smile.

"You two are behaving like an old married couple."
Even at Paula's jest, the two refused to waver from gazing into each other's eyes. Was Audrey even paying attention?

"Oh, yes... right you are Paula. Anyone feel like waltzing!"

Audrey's sudden outburst was result of her love sickness for Alister. Paula, and anyone else for that matter, could see that from a mile away. The young couple drifted

back into the crowd, arm in arm, leaving
Paula to dwell.

"Well, that was interesting...?" Thomas
said, laughing clumsily.

Paula didn't respond right away and only
watched the many couples dancing.

"Those two are chasing each other's
tails a bit too much, don't you think,
mistress?"

"It appears that way, Fulton."

Taking note of the unhappiness behind the
girl's demeanour, the butler lifted his lady's
hand and bowed.

"Care to dance with me, mistress?"

Without waiting for an answer,
Thomas weaved the girl through the crowd,
one hand upon hers, the other around her
waist. He tapped his feet back and forth to
the orchestra, one foot in, one foot out, then
he elegantly twirled the girl. Paula was very
familiar with this dance, the waltz. Somehow
it was different, the way Thomas moved... it
was captivating, dangerously flawless, you
could almost say it was other-worldly...

"What's the matter, mistress... I can
feel your heart beating wildly..."

Paula's eyes widened as the butler moved his
face close to her ear.

"You know, there's no need for you to feel jealous of anyone."

"How did you"-

The man interrupted Paula's question and stared into her eyes.

"I just know, I feel like I've known you forever mistress..."

Thomas propped forward, his breath tickling Paula's silky lips. The girl subtly looked around the room. If anyone so much shifted their heads in their direction a scandal would arise overnight. A mistress and her butler, it was forbidden, it was shameful, it was... so amorous...

"Thomas..."

The lady tightened her grip on the man's shoulders, her eyes went soft and her voice stifled.

"I"-

"Look out, Lady Audrey!"

The peace of the moment was broken when unexpected gunshots rang out across the ballroom, making everyone scream and scarper for their lives. In a blur, Agatha ran across the hall and rammed Audrey out the way, just as the colossal glass chandelier above, fell to the ground with a deafening shatter.

"Agatha!" Audrey screamed.

Agatha lay under the fragmented debris, gasping silently. With her final breath she murmured the words "*mistress...*". Tears streamed down Audrey's checks as she ran outside into the garden. Paula was going to run after her when five more gunshots rained down upon the room. Looking around to the upper balcony, Paula caught sight of a shadowy figure wearing a long black coat and mask. The figure shook their head over the whole scene, then sprinted behind an upstairs wall. Fury bubbling inside of her, the lady ran up the steps in pursuit of the perpetrator.

"Mistress, no!"

Thomas followed Paula's movements and ran to the manor's higher levels. Everyone around him was bellowing, crying and stumbling over each other in a frenzy. He wanted to help them but couldn't stop, in that moment getting his mistress to safety was the only thing that mattered. Paula turned a corner and found herself standing face-to-face with the culprit. The figure cocked his head. Even though he was wearing a jester's mask, Paula knew he was eyeing her prudently. Thomas darted around the wall and stood directly in front of his mistress. As soon as the perpetrator saw Thomas, he drew his gun.

The culprit pulled the trigger, only to unleash a flurry of hollow snaps. He had emptied all six cartridges. With another disfigured twist to his head, the killer jumped out of an unlocked window and vanished into the stillness of the night. Standing in shock to what she just witnessed, Paula only snapped to her senses when Thomas shook her shoulders.

"My lady! We need to go!"

The young woman's pupils wavered and her throat went abnormally dry. Yet again they had fallen into the murderer's callous ploy. Like insects in a spider's web, they had been caught.

*

Three weeks had passed since the masquerade massacre. Ten people were reported dead, including the faithful maid, Agatha Turner. Seventeen people were injured, not so much from bullets, but instead from the chandelier's glass shards and from being trampled. Amongst the casualties, two people were missing; Duke Alister Knox and Viscount Landers. The police investigated the crime scene shortly after Paula's frightful encounter. They found no other open doors or windows, except for the front entrance and the window the criminal escaped from. The investigation would have been a waste if it weren't for one of the officers stumbling upon an empty pistol cartridge not too far from the manor's gardens.

The officers took statements from everyone who attended the ball. Audrey was far too hysterical to answer the questions clearly, but Paula stepped in where she could. Unsurprisingly, the officers were more concerned with Paula's chance encounter and on that basis made a sketch of the lady's description of the culprit. After taking a sketch of a skinny, dark attired individual, the press got involved and dubbed the criminal *Twisted Jester.* The title was fitting for him since the character was typically seen wearing a black and white jesters mask and often angled his head devilishly to the sight of mayhem. The recollection still gave Paula shivers. After the statements were given, the officers started a full-scale investigation regarding the disappearance of Alister Knox and Viscount Landers, as well as placing law enforcing teams around London's darkest alleys. Everyone was hopeful this movement would ward the Jester off but the Ethel household was not so sure.

Christa and Clement were distressed from the news they received that night. When Paula returned and told them about the evening's appalling events they broke out into tears and refused to let go of the girl. Since then, the servants kept an exceptionally close eye on their mistress. After all, the three of them would be nothing without her.

Paula sat in her study, facing a fresh pile of letters and documents. There was a letter from Audrey discussing how troubled she was over Agatha's passing and over Alister's uncanny vanishing. They mourned over the maid's short-lived life, but none of them could get their heads around Alister's case. Where on earth could he be? Audrey tried not to think of the worst and instead waited daily to hear good news from the search parties. After sending a reply to Audrey, Paula went back to the manor's library. All the tension was weighing heavily on her and only one thing could distract her fragile heart from it all; getting lost in another world.

Searching amongst the high shelves, Paula found exactly what she was seeking out. It was a book that was written some years before her birth. At the time she found it she was too young to understand the plot or terminology it comprised of, but now that she was older she could finally understand its concepts. The book told a forbidden tale about two childhood lovers who struggled to surpass the problems society threw at them. One of them was part of the bourgeoisie and the other, a proletariat striving to fit-in with high society. At times it was bitter, at times it was sweet, but the reason Paula adored the book to such an extent was because of its author. It was Jacob who'd written this novel. Reading the tale made the young woman feel closer to him somehow and reminded her of the good life she once lived. The silence was broken when the library door was suddenly pushed open.

"My lady, I thought you might be in here."

Paula's expression softened. Three months... that's all it took for Thomas to memorise his schedule, familiarise himself with the property and get to know all his mistress's affable habits. The man sat at the opposite side of the table, analysing the book's exterior.

"*That day in Autumn*? I don't believe I've read this one."

Thomas scanned the book's title and author. He was amazed to see Jacob was the creator of the novel. He recalled the day Paula interviewed him, she told him about the previous Ethel butler and about how remarkable he was. Now that Thomas thought about it, he didn't know much about Jacob Lockhart...

"I didn't know Mr Lockhart wrote a book?"
Paula lowered the book and looked over to her butler.

"This was Jacob's first and only novel."
"Oh? Please do tell why."

Paula enlightened the butler on the bitter-sweet romance novel, he was charmed by the complex storyline and pleasant ending. The girl showed Thomas a photograph of the late butler which was plastered at the end of the book's pages. Wavy light brown hair, gemstone eyes and a tidy uniform that somehow looked better than Thomas' own clothing. How could a man with almost the same colour eyes as him, almost the same colour hair and uniform look so much better than him? '*It must be his commitment to the task,*' Thomas thought to himself. After talking of Jacob's writings, the two went on to discuss the Ethel's history.

"So, how did Mr Lockhart become the family butler?"

Leaning further onto the table, Paula dropped into a whisper. The droplets of rain sputtered and spat against the window, making it impossible for ravenous ears to catch a single word. As if noticing the invisible spies, Thomas also propped his ear closer. It was almost like the two were playing a game of childish whispers.

"Well, both my mother and Jacob were in education together. Mother studied business and Jacob was fascinated with literature. After they graduated, mother told Jacob the news... she was to be wed." Thomas straightened his back and held in a breath-waiting for Paula's next words.

"It would be no mistake to say Jacob was stunned, he could never imagine parting from his good friend and so, he began training to become a butler." Paula whipped her head left and right then parted her lips to finish the tale.

"Within a couple of months, Jacob had completed his training and was on his way to becoming a fully-fledged butler. Naturally, mother hired him since he was now qualified and still her loyal friend..." The girl looked away.

"And the rest... well, you know how the story ends."

Supporting his head on the chair, Thomas let out a stammered breath. He was behaving as if he just ran a hundred-mile marathon.

"My lady... the way you tell stories, it will have the audience on the edge of their seats!"

The lady chuckled at the statement, but only for a minute.

"You know, I'm glad mother and Jacob were friends, if they hadn't been, I would have never learned about the pleasures of reading, the art of piano, or the serenity of nature."

The man observed Paula closely and contemplated his next words.

"Mistress you are very special, it may have been Jacob who helped you discover yourself, but I know you would have been just as talented, elegant and kind no matter what."

The girl's cheeks flushed pink at the compliments, Thomas knew exactly what to say in every situation. It occurred to her that in all the months that passed the butler did not just carve a pathway to success... he also carved a pathway to her heart.

*

Paula entered the kitchen to the sound of a music box. The tune 'London Bridge is falling down' played on repeat, but no matter how much she searched, she could not find the box anywhere. The light of the moon looked slightly green as it shone down on the tabletop, lighting up the quaint little tea party set upon it. A selection of biscuits, sponge cake, a variety of teas and two little rabbit toys sat waiting, angled in a way that looked like they were staring at the girl.

Paula took a seat at the end of the table, the biscuits in front of her floating right into her hands.

"More tea, my dear?" A devilish voice came from in front of her.

There the Jester stood, pouring Earl Grey into a floating tea cup. He laughed maniacally, the tea overflowing onto the table, never-ending. It turned red, making everything around it change to crimson. The biscuits in Paula's hands turned to ash, and as she screamed, the Jester was suddenly behind her, pushing a dagger into the small of her back...

Paula awoke in a fright. She scanned her bedroom and noticed her window was left sightly open and her old music box was lying on the floor. She locked the window, and set the music box back down on her bedside before climbing back into bed and hugging her quilt tightly.

"Thomas will be here by morning... Thomas will be here by morning..." she quietly chanted, falling back asleep to the thought of her butler.

Chapter 8

The suspicion

The morning sun parted the clouds, causing a beam of light to spread across Paula's four-poster bed. Her eyelids still felt heavy but with some effort and the prompt of the door creaking, she gradually fluttered them open.

"Mph, good morning... Thomas," she yawned.

He chuckled, "Good morning, mistress. Sleep pleasantly?"

"Mmm... something like that," she replied.

The girl stretched and yawned a bit more as the butler ripped the curtains apart and poured a cup of her favourite Earl Gray. She watched him pour it carefully just to make sure she was indeed awake. She sighed under her breath as she realised she wasn't dreaming.

Paula had become extremely reliant on her butler and was abashed to say she was becoming increasingly lethargic. Thomas demonstrated his capacity, and as promised his duties now centred around Paula's needs; this included getting her dressed, combing her hair, brushing her teeth and going above and beyond to make sure she was healthy and content. It would take some more time and effort but gradually the two were getting comfortable with each other's presence.

Paula's grandmother also paid them a visit after hearing about the masquerade episode. She took the time to console her granddaughter and get acquainted with Thomas properly. Ophelia was impressed with Paula's impeccable choice and went so far as to say the girl chose as good as she did (Clement and Christa were pleased about this too). No one, however, was more grateful than Thomas. After all this time he finally got his life back on track. The man had respectable friends, a lovable mistress and an extravagant home. But his greatest wish still lingered, he wanted peace to return to London and the Twisted Jester to be caught.

"Time to get dressed for breakfast, my lady."

Pushing the duvet off her body, the young woman sat up and dangled her legs over the bedside. Holding a change of clothes, Thomas slipped off his mistress' nightgown and buttoned her into a frilly navy-blue dress.

"For today my lady, Clement and myself have prepared porridge accompanied with cuts of sliced ham and asparagus. After breakfast we must finish reading *Macbeth* and it seems we have the afternoon free."

Paula nodded, though she did not seem completely engaged in her butler's words. Since the weather was getting nippier, Thomas placed Paula's feet atop his knees and pulled a pair of cotton socks along her legs. The young woman blushed as the man tied a thin suspender belt around her thighs-securing the socks so they wouldn't sag to the bottom of her ankles. Somehow, looking down at her butler's mesmerising eyes made her chest tighten.

*

The 'free afternoon' Thomas had spoken of came sooner than expected and by 2 o'clock the family was sitting in the living room. As usual Thomas and Clement made an exceptional breakfast, and Christa cleared the light snow dusting all the doors and windows. The bulk of the chores and Paula's further reading was complete, so everyone went about filling their idol time.

"Checkmate!" Said Christa.

"Huh? Already?"

Clement scratched his head. Christa beat him for the third time in a row! Surely the gardener was not always this good at chess?

"Say Christa... how'd you get so good?"

The blonde gardener gave a little fluttery wave to Thomas who was sitting on the settee opposite them. The butler brought a hand to his mouth and chortled when seeing Clement's muddled expression.

"Oi, that's not fair! Thomas taught you how to play! Come on mate, teach me somethin' too!"

"No Thomas. If you tell him all the tricks, then he'll trounce me for sure!"

At this point even Paula looked up from her newspaper, amused by the servant's antics.

"What if Thomas opposes the both of you? Surely combining your techniques will be an advantage," Paula suggested.

The two servants eyed each other cynically, then, with a movement so quick, shook hands and nodded. Paula hummed a tune under her breath as if she were congratulating herself for carrying out a strenuous mission or something far greater. The peace of the moment made the girl feel warm. The feeling was short lived. Turning the paper, she gasped when Viscount Landers' photograph was printed on the page. His body was surrounded by hedges and withered flowers, on closer inspection Paula recognised where this photo was taken. It was Audrey's garden maze! The old man's body was warped into a bizarre shape, left in the centre of the maze like a cruel prize waiting to be found.

"What's the matter, mistress?" All three servants spoke up at once.

"It's... it's Viscount Landers... he's dead."

Taking the paper from Paula's shaking hand, Thomas read it silently. He went pale and handed the paper to Clement and Christa. Failing to read the room, Clement blurted out the headline:

'Landers' body found in Young's estate!'

'No one could have imagined Viscount Lander's sudden passing, but to everyone's horror, the elderly man's body was found in the centre of Miss Audrey Young's garden maze! Unlike the other recent murders, Landers had red marks around his neck, he

been chocked to death and left to the callous hands of Mother Nature. It leaves some to speculate... was the murder a coincidence... could the Jester be to blame...or is it all part of the nobles secret ploy? Police interrogation is currently underway. Miss Audrey Young, as well numerous other nobles are being questioned, with any hope, all will be revealed soon.'

"Clement!" Christa slapped the man's arm, "You're upsetting the mistress!"

"Ow, s-sorry my lady- I didn't mea-"

"Clement, it's alright." Thomas silenced the room.

Paula looked to the floor. No one knew what to think... the murder could not be a coincidence, and how dare they poke fingers at Audrey! It was obvious that the Jester was behind this crime, it was just rotten luck no one could prove it.

It was clear at this point that the crazed Jester was targeting nobles and eradicating them ruthlessly.

"This is bloody ridiculous! Why can't this Twisted Jester be caught already?" said Christa, face red and fists clenched.

Never before did the household witness Christa's wrath. The woman was always so calm and collected, seeing her in this state was frightening to say the least. Clement reached out a comforting hand only to be pushed away.

"Please, Clement!"

Christa raged on. A flicker of guilt washed over her when she swatted Clement's hand away, but instead of apologising she ran off outside. The chef was stunned-as if an arrow had pierced deep into his being. With a shake of his head he looked to Thomas then marched into the kitchen.

"We better give them some time to themselves, Thomas."

Paula's voice broke the thickened atmosphere. The lady resumed reading the paper, hoping there were no more nasty shocks ahead. Thomas let out a sigh, then began to clear away the game of chess. Both kings lay flat on the board, surrounded by nothing, not even a single pawn. Surrendering your king is the biggest symbol of failure, but what happens when two kings fall at the same time? Do they both prevail or is it simply an all-out annihilation? Somehow, not even Thomas knew the real answer.

*

The morning sun transformed into a purple distortion as afternoon, and then evening rolled around. Clement and Thomas had prepared dinner but Christa still hadn't returned from her little tantrum. Paula pressed her palms against the window, peering out into the darkness.

"I cannot see her out there," she said. Thomas threw on an overcoat and trekked outside the front gate. He checked around the manor's entrance and did a full-circle around the property. He looked left to the overgrown grove; he looked right to the frosted fields... Christa was nowhere in sight. With a shake of his head, he returned to the manor.

"She isn't outside of the estate; she must be somewhere within the manor's fences."

"Oh, Christa..." Paula frowned.

Clement, who had been sitting in the corner of the room did not seem so worried. He looked out into the garden, visible irritation on his face.

"Tch... who does she think she is... leading us on a wild goose chase."

Clement mumbled that under his breath, only loud enough for the dust bunnies to hear him. He watched Thomas and Paula who were scampering in and out of the kitchen and hallways like mad sniffer dogs. This was not helping anyone, they needed to go out *there*, into the ugly darkness of the night.

"Mistress, we should look in the garden. We'll find her quicker if we split up."

The chef mustered up the courage to make his voice heard. It was obvious the gardener was sulking somewhere in the garden, it only made logical sense to split up and search for her there.

"Very well, Clement. You and I shall go, the mistress will stay here."

"No, Thomas. I want to help."

"But, my lady"-

"We do not have time for this!" said Paula, while marching to the back entrance of the manor.

"We will find her quicker, together."

Paula wrapped a shawl around herself and opened the door to the garden. A gust of wind blew in a bit of snow, the biting cold only now setting in.

"Right, myself and the mistress will look around the orchard. Clement, you search by the greenhouse."

Thomas and Paula took off to the far end of the garden, it was possible Christa was seeking refuge in the many tight, well-hidden areas of shrubbery. Clement went in the opposite direction, where the slumbering flowerbeds and greenhouse sat.

It was alarming to see how different the garden looked in winter. The chef wished he had the light of the basking summer sun, and the feeling of thick grass hugging his ankles. Instead, he was lashed at by the winter wind and kissed by the drops of falling snow. The frost crunched like bones under his desperate trudges, it made him feel rather uneasy. Hearing a noise resonating in the darkness, Clement spun around to see an owl flying overhead. Suddenly, he remembered Christa's fear of barn owls[6]. He was surprised the girl hadn't gotten spooked and called it quits, being out here was far more eerie than anything.

"Christa... where'd you go?"

A clatter came from the greenhouse. The hairs on the back of the man's neck stood in such a way that he resembled a struggling hedgehog. Pondering a little, the

---

[6] Victorians often thought owls were ghosts until the creatures were properly identified as birds.

chef concluded that the noise maker was either Christa or someone far more sinister. No matter how terrified he was, it was part of a servant's job to protect the manor. This was either going to be the bravest decision of his life or the most foolish...

Plastering himself against the greenhouse's outer walls, Clement peeked inside. Despite there being a low light source coming from inside the structure, Clement couldn't really see anything as the coniferous saplings had been shifted along the window benches. He crept closer to the ajar door. Sucking-in his stomach, the man shuffled through the gap, he was relieved to see Christa crouched on the floor. There were a bunch of empty plant pots and a small oil lamp by her side. Her clothes and hair were littered with soil and pine needles and she was scrubbing away the debris of broken pottery.

"Wood!"

The startled gardener scrambled backwards into the mess she was cleaning.

"Morris?"

Clement fell to his knees and wrapped his arms around the girl. Christa was motionless for a second, then, with a sigh, she buried her head into the man's shoulder.

"Oh Clement, I'm sorry for lashing out at you so rudely."
The man pulled back and stared at the gardener wide-eyed.

"I'm angrier at the fact you ran off without warning!"
Feeling a bit sheepish, Christa comprehended all the trouble she had caused.

"Ah...yes, I'm sorry about running away and for being so stubborn, and making you fret over me."

After a lengthy apology, Clement could not help but chuckle a little. He was still hugging onto the woman and didn't seem to mind that pine needles and dirt were sticking to his coat.

"Christa..."
The man affectionately stroked his thumb against the girl's cheek, ridding her of a mud stain in the process.

"...What a mess you are."

"It's not my fault! First, I had a fit over that damn Jester, then I decided to organise the saplings to calm down, but I slipped over the melted snow and smashed the mistress's best pot on the floor...making this mess. And, after all that, you frightened me and now I'm a bloody state too"-

"Do you ever stop yappin'...?"

Closing the distance between them, Clement grazed his lips against the blonde's forehead and kissed her warmly. Christa felt hot tears prick her eyes, she always knew Clement cared about her but why did he always make it so sappy. Giving him another squeeze, the two sat buried in each other's warmth for a while.

*

On the other side of the garden, Paula and Thomas were driving themselves insane looking for the lost gardener.

"Aw, Thomas! Where could she be?"

It must have been the hundredth time Paula asked that question, and Thomas still hadn't a good answer. The tips of Paula's nose and ears were crimson; the cold was gradually getting to her. If they didn't find Christa soon, Thomas worried his mistress would faint from exhaustion.

"Mistress, we should check with Clement and see if he has found her."

With a sneeze and a shiver, Paula agreed, but only on the condition that they investigate the entirety of the orchard first. Marching ahead, Paula's outline could scarcely be seen in the rolling mist. Thomas didn't appreciate the idea of her running around in the dead-of-night with a deranged killer on the loose, but then again, he didn't like the idea of Christa being out here on her own either.

"AAAHHHH!"

Paula howled like a distressed wolf in the night. Thomas' heart rate instantly accelerated. It couldn't be... there's no way his mistress of all people fell upon misfortune.

"MISTRESS!"

The butler sprinted into the fog, only guided by his mistress's cries. Each leap caused his stomach to lurch, he felt like he was gagging on air.

"Please, please be alright..."

When the butler eventually reached his mistress' side, she was backed up against a barren tree, staring in dismay at the hunched imp-like figure sprawled at her feet. Thomas took a hold of Paula's hand and pulled her close to his chest. The person on the floor made a chocking sound, like he was gargling his own saliva... or worse. With vigilance, Thomas offered his hand to the distressed being. The figure looked up at them making Paula screech.

"Duke Alister...?"

The both of them hauled Alister to his feet and positioned him to the faint light of the moon. His eyes were bruised and puffy, and his lips looked like they had been inflicted with poison ivy. The man tried to speak, but no words came out. He coughed up saliva which dribbled from the side of his lips, blood from a gash on his head also oozed down his neck, staining his white shirt a dangerous crimson.

"We need to call a doctor!" Thomas said.

After struggling to get Alister to the manor, Thomas fiddled with the phone and managed to dial the physician's number. From hearing the urgency in Thomas' voice, the doctor pledged to make haste.

The time spent waiting for help was one of the worst things Paula had endured. Observing Alister's distressing behaviour was saddening and rather disturbing. It was a wonder Clement found Christa and came back to the manor in time, otherwise Paula would be dealing with far too many stresses at once.

"Clement! Fetch some water, would you?"

The chef ran and filled a glass. Paula tried directing Alister's lips to the drink, but more water was dribbling out of his mouth than going in.

"Christa, get a handkerchief!"

Christa was midway pulling a handkerchief from her pocket, when Alister put his beaten hands over Paula's and blinked. It seems like his teary hues were saying 'give up'. The girl began to cry, not in pain, not in anguish, but in sympathy. The sympathy that compelled her to weep over others misfortune. She didn't know Alister, not really, yet all she could do was weep for him.

Suddenly everyone in the room looked pained. Christa latched onto Clement. Thomas covered half of his face with his gloves, not wanting his mistress to see him with teary eyes.

*

Half an hour passed and the doctor arrived at the manor. With a check-up, the doctor took the decision to take Alister to the infirmary; austere treatment needed to be given for the man's survival. Before the doctor set off with Alister, Paula walked out into the snow and questioned him.

"Doctor, can you tell me what happened to the duke?"

The man adjusted his white coat and eyed his surroundings shiftily.

"I shouldn't be telling you this but... it was cyanide poisoning..."

"What"-

Even though the doctor claimed he couldn't disclose any information, he continued his analysis as if he were having a Sunday gossip.

"Cyanide poisoning is lethal, with a large enough dose the victim would be dead in a couple of hours, however... whoever gave the dose to Mr Knox knew exactly what he was doing, he only gave enough to disable the man, not kill him."

Paula stared in a state of disbelief. There was no doubt this was the Jester's doing! Only he could have thought of doing something so evil. Hurting people just for his sadistic pleasures... it was utterly diabolical.

"Well, thank you doctor. Please take care of Duke Knox."

With a brief bow and a swing of his white coat the doctor climbed into the coach and took the sleeping Alister with him. Thinking about the night's events made Paula feel nauseous, how much more could she loose? Thomas looked at his mistress' fatigued expression and frowned.

"Mistress, you should get some rest," said Thomas.
Thomas looked to the other two heavy eyed servants.

"In fact, we should all get some rest."

Christa and Clement did not need further persuading. They dragged their lead-like legs across the hall to their quarters, yawning and whining in-sync with one another. Thomas walked behind Paula up the stairs, somehow his demeanour seemed off; like he was putting up some sort of front. Yet, Paula felt it wasn't the time or place to question it.

Once the girl was in the security of her own room, she watched Thomas prepare a fluffy towel and nightgown. Still not enquiring about his frown, the girl went into the bathroom and locked the door behind her. She nestled into her already prepared bath and closed her eyes. Eric, Baron Keith, Landers, Alister... they were all of noble blood, but what else...? They were all male... and Paula couldn't recall purposeful killings of women. But, if the Twisted Jester was only targeting noblemen then why didn't he injure half of the people at the ball? The whole occurrence muddled the jigsaw. The Jester's devious mind could not be compared with that of a sane man, or with Paula's naïve thinking. She could not think of a logical reason for all his madness.

Looking at her hands, the girl realised she was evolving into a raisin. She exhaled into the lukewarm water before heaving herself up. As soon as she treaded on the floor, realisation hit her, Thomas had her towel...

Putting her head against the locked door, she called out to her butler.

"Thomas, close your eyes, would you?"

"Why, mistress?"

Water dripped off Paula's breasts, forming a puddle on the once spotless floor.

"I haven't got a towel!"

With an edge of annoyance in her voice, she hugged her body with her arms (as if that were really going to warm her up).

"Whatever you say, mistress."

When hearing his muffled response, Paula breathed a sigh of relief and unlocked the door. Thomas was standing in the centre of the room, eyes closed tight, arm outstretched clutching a warm towel. Even though his eyes were closed, Paula felt embarrassed... she was standing completely bare, with only ten inches of space between her and Thomas... A MAN. With a moment's hesitation, Paula took the towel and patted her soaked tresses. She tried to dry the trickling water on her back but failed miserably.

"Umm, Thomas... I don't suppose you could dry me off...?"

The brunette man blushed. Honestly, was the mistress becoming so dependent on him that she could not even dry herself properly?

"Let me guess... I still can't open my eyes?"

"I'm afraid not, my dear butler."

Smiling to himself, Thomas reached out a hand and found his palms against the towel's warm surface.

"I accept your challenge, mistress."

When feeling Thomas rub her back, Paula flinched slightly but managed to compose herself just as quickly. It was ridiculous that such a small gesture was making the woman's skin hot. She claimed to be a capable adult, but her fantasies were that of an over-imaginative adolescent. Failing to control her emotions, she decided changing the atmosphere would be for the better-the last thing she wanted was to ruin her and Thomas' relationship over her ludicrous daydreams.

"Thomas?"

Still drying her skin with closed eyes, Thomas replied with a simple hum.

"You have not been yourself lately, have you?"

The notion caught the butler completely off guard and in a panic the man opened his eyes.

Like a rabbit being stalked by a fox, the girl knew Thomas was watching her. Paula did not dare turn around, instead she cast a pout over the side of her shoulder. Thomas ineptly passed the girl her nightgown and turned himself in the opposite direction.

"I should have known you would notice."

While Paula slipped on her nightgown, the butler began speaking his mind.

"I'm not feeling like myself because... I failed you."

Not saying anything Paula stood still, back-to-back with her butler.

"I let you run off in the fog, I let you go off on your own. It was fortunate you met Mr Knox and not that damn Jester! I wanted to protect you, and so far, I haven't done an impeccable job."

All of a sudden Thomas felt two arms around his back.

"Thomas, I forbid you to say such things. All you've been doing is protecting me. You saved me at the ball, and came to my rescue in the fog. Even if I run off, even if I am in trouble, I won't worry because I know you will come and save me."

"Mistress..."

Holding the girl's hand in his own, the man turned around and leaned his forehead against Paula's damp hair. Paula tried not to look her butler in the eyes, failing miserably. With some hesitation, the two finally gave-in and pressed their lips together. The kiss was so overwhelming the girl felt warm tears in her eyes. Thomas pulled away. Narrowing his gaze, he observed Paula's expression and then kissed her again and again. This was real, his mistress was safe in his arms; alive and well. Thomas didn't want to lose her to the hands of anyone... not again. He made a promise there and then, he would protect her till the end of time.

Chapter 9

Witnesses

The servants bustled around the kitchen, brewing tea, boiling eggs and searing bread. Even with all the gruesome affairs going on, they still had their duties to carry out. The whistle of the kettle caught Thomas off guard; he glanced around as though he heard the murmurs of a ghost. The other servants had never taken him to be the oblivious sort. They both looked his way for a second, then continued with their work as if nothing happened. Ignoring the odd looks he received from the chef and gardener, Thomas reached the top cupboard where all the elaborate china was kept. He took out the blue and white Wedgwood set and plated the sweets and brew as if he was an expert confectioner. With a proud puff of his chest he carried the tray to the dining room. When he was out of earshot, the other two servants began conspiring.

"What'd you suppose has gotten into Thomas?" Clement asked.

"Hmm, you know, I'm not too sure..."

Christa peeked her head around the door's edge, the chef following-suit. Thomas was rubbing the back of his neck sheepishly, while Paula complemented the grand presentation of her morning appetisers.

Clement's jaw dropped, "Of course the mistress is impressed, she loves the fancy teacups!"

"No you ninny, it's not just about the teacups! Look at the way they're behaving..."

Clement squinted as if he were trying on a pair of spectacles, he looked at Paula, then at Thomas. The man stared at them until an idea struck him.

"They're...they're... best mates!" The gardener threw daggers with her stare, making the chef recoil and re-think his conclusion.

"They're not best mates...?"

The brunet man blurted out any old nonsense. Christa sighed, and resumed toasting a piece of bread.

"The roses are blooming..." the girl whispered under her breath.

Clement didn't catch her revelation and went back to watching the eggs boil.

Still chatting with Paula, Thomas described each sweet treat laid out on the table. Paula tasted each confectionery, savouring every delicate flavour that came over her. There was a slice of charlotte cake, a butter biscuit, a circular cream tart, and a malt-chocolate bob-bon. Different aromas kissed the girl's nose, the slight acidic touch of the tart, the chocolatey smoothness of the bon-bon, it was all so exquisite.

"You've outdone yourself yet again, Thomas."

"You flatter me, mistress."

After the delicious delicacies were no more, Paula retreated to her study. It was the end of the month, and that meant it was time to post donations to the workhouse.

After Earl Randal's passing the workhouse was in ruin. No one except the runners of the organisation knew it was actually the Randal family who contributed the most funds. Naturally, Paula was going to play her part too. The Ethel's also had a generous reputation and the girl intended to keep it that way. After sealing a letter and some shillings in an envelope, the girl signed it with her name and family crest.

Next was evaluating the family business; *Ethel's Tea House* had been running for almost thirty years. It was established by her grandfather and then taken over by her father. It was odd to her that she was suddenly overseeing all the company's affairs, but she needed to embrace change. Paula had managers in place who watched over the many shops around London and received monthly reports on how well the tea was selling. Her favourite part of managing the business was experimenting with new flavours of tea and occasionally making sweets to go with them. It was amusing; sometimes she visited one of the shops at random and surprised the guests. That certainly got them in high spirits.

"My lady! There's a telephone call for you," Christa said.

Christa leaned in the doorway with a worried expression etched on her face. With a quick movement Paula went downstairs to where Thomas was holding the phone.

"It's Miss Young," he whispered.

Placing the phone to her ear, Paula was both relieved and saddened to hear Audrey on the other end. Her voice was urgent and panicked; the constant stuttering was making it exceedingly difficult for Paula to understand her. After urging Audrey to calm down, the lady managed to get a decent conversation out of her. Alister Knox had been discharged from hospital, and sent to Young's estate. From the moment he came

127

to Audrey's manor, he had been rambling about something; the only problem was no one could decipher his speech as the cyanide was still in effect. Audrey wanted Paula to pay her a visit, maybe together they could figure out what Alister was trying to say.

"What is it, my lady?"

"We need to depart to Young's estate immediately."

Without giving much of an explanation, Paula hauled on her coat and scarf and left Christa and Clement to tend to the manor. Thomas beckoned the coach from the driveway and within a few moments they were off to Audrey's estate once again.

"Mistress, can you please tell me what's going on?"

The girl explained Audrey's predicament while Thomas listened with nervous ears.

"So, Miss Young needs your help translating Mr Knox's speech?"

"In short, yes."

Both of them thought about many things on the coach ride; most of it was centred around the Twisted Jester's devious actions, and fear of who he'd strike next. The sloppy mix of rain and snow slurred against the windows and the wind's slender fingers slid through the crevasses of the doors. Paula shivered. When the weather became frightful, she couldn't help but ponder about all the tragedies that befell her. The girl wondered why the Jester did such a thing to Alister; instead of murdering him, they just let him go. Perhaps Alister inflicted some sort of hurt on the Jester, causing him to flee? Or perhaps the insane murderer just let him escape purposefully? Getting answers from Alister was everyone's best lead. He may not be able to speak, but there must be some way to get his insight across.

The horses came to a standstill once reaching Audrey's manor. Mud scrapped against their tired hooves and steam jetted from their nostrils. Cliffe calmed them and called out:

"We've arrived, Miss Paula."

Paula tugged her scarf tighter around her neck. Thomas stuck very close to the girl's heels; being in the same location that the Jester was once in disgusted him. Upon reaching the front entrance, Paula was reminded of the masquerade ball, and how Agatha was there to greet them.

"Thank you for coming so soon, Paula," Audrey rushed to the door, embracing her friend tightly before summoning the two inside.

It was Thomas' nightmare to see dust and muck in every corner of the manor. It was obvious that Audrey wasn't in her best days, losing Agatha was clearly weighing heavily on her. When the three finally reached the dining room, the lighting was oddly dim and the atmosphere was unusually heavy. Alister sat with his eyes closed, head engulfed in the settee, there were heavy bags under his eyes and parts of his face were still bruised. There was a man sitting next to him, Paula recognised him as Archie; a man she briefly saw at the ball.

"I took the liberty of bringing Earl Archie Stitch along, as he is Alister's most trusted friend."

Paula hadn't the faintest idea Alister was acquainted with Archie, but then again, how could she; being trapped like a songbird for most of her life caused her to be behind in recent affairs. Alister's eyes slowly edged open, he rolled his head over and looked at everyone with watery eyes.

"Thank goodness your finally awake, my love."

Alister stared at Audrey and a flicker of familiarity crossed him. It looked like it took him all his might, but he managed to muster a faint smile. He turned his head slowly to Paula and his pupils broadened. Alister pointed and shook his head at the lady and her butler.

"I think he remembers something!"

Archie took a piece of parchment and a quill out of his pocket and sat it down in front of the agitated man.

"Do you think you could try writing it, ol' chap?"

The man calmed down a little and tried to write. He clumsily lifted the pen's inky nib to the paper and dropped it after forming a few indecipherable letters. It was pointless, he couldn't hold the pen long enough to write full sentences. He took the quill in his left hand and attempted to write again. Paula could see the struggle on his face.

"If you can't write it, try drawing it instead," Paula suggested.

It looked like the man was going to cry; how frustrating it must be to want to say something so desperately and not be able to.

"Take your time, my love."

With some encouragement from Audrey, the man scrawled down some lines on the paper. Everyone in the room watched in silence as the lines became sharper. Alister's hand fell, and the quill's ink spluttered on the page. Archie lifted the sketch, and examined it.

"It looks like a fancy clock?" Alister's eyelids dropped, and once again he grew sleepy.

"Rest now, my darling," Audrey tearily caressed her lover's cheek.

The rest of the group gathered around the drawing and tried to make sense of it.

"It could be an antique... that squiggle looks a bit like the branding *Bridgedale* used to do?" Paula reckoned.

"It's a pocket watch."

The confidence in Thomas' voice made the other three inspect the sketch again. It took a lot of careful interpretation, but one could make out a chain, and a spherical shaped lid with a boarder. There was also a peculiar marking engraved on the lid of the pocket watch, three squiggly lines.

"It's all well and good we have a theory, but what on earth does it mean?"

Archie had a good point. None of them had a clue what the pocket watch object meant, but it was better than nothing at all.

"Audrey, may I take this sketch with me?"

"Of course, Paula,"

"I'll investigate this further and hopefully bring you some good news."

After Paula tucked the drawing away in her coat pocket, she and Thomas said their goodbyes and left for the front door. Audrey was miserable that Paula was departing from her so soon, but knowing her dear friend, she suspected the young woman was formulating some sort of plan. Before they left the manor, Archie saw them off, it looked as though he wanted to get something off his chest. Archie reached for Paula's shoulder and parted his mouth to speak. Something odd must have possessed him, as no sooner did he open his mouth did he close it shut again. Paula enquired about it, but the blonde just shook his head-retracting any of his earlier actions.

About halfway into the carriage journey home, Thomas couldn't help but ask what their next moves were going to be.

"Do you think we did enough to help, my lady?"

Paula thought carefully. Given the situation and the short amount of time they had, she believed they did a good job; especially considering they got some information out of Alister.

"I think we did all we can for now. But I do believe we need to delve deeper into this pocket watch business."

"What do you have in mind?" Thomas asked.

"Taking the sketch to *Bridgedale* would be our best option," Paula said.

The butler turned his own pocket watch over in his hands. He realised that not all the designs were the same.

When the carriage arrived back to the Ethel estate two police officers were standing outside of the entrance. One of the officers tapped his baton against the coach door.

"You're Miss Paula Ethel, correct?" The girl stepped out; clearly stunned.

"Yes, I'm Paula Ethel."

"We need to have a word with you, miss."

One of the officers coughed and glanced in Thomas' direction.

"In private."

Paula shifted her eyes. Thomas wandered to the manor where the other two servants were looking-out like curious puppies. The man didn't feel right leaving Paula on her own, not even with the police. If she didn't give the indication of her being fine, the man would have stayed, even if the officers were against it.

"What seems to be the problem, sir?"

"We just have some questions, miss. It has come to our attention that a murder occurred in your family eight years ago, correct?"

Paula became increasingly shakier as the officers mentioned her family's demise, but did her best to appear unstirred.

"Yes, there was an accident over Stone-Arch bridge some years ago."

"I see. Well, we have a theory that the recent murder cases have something to do with that accident."

Suddenly, Paula paid full attention.

"What...?"

"Now, we haven't sufficient evidence to prove this for certain, but with your cooperation..."

The officer handed her a card with a number, and a file containing information about Audrey's ball and that fateful day. The other officer adjusted his hat, visibly uncomfortable from talking about such a sensitive topic.

"Keep in touch Miss Paula, your help will be greatly appreciated."

With a swing of their batons, the pair were on their way, completely unaware of the horrors they made the girl recall.

"Mistress!"

All three servants arose from their work when their mistress entered the living room. Thomas could see from a mile away that something was off.

"Are you alright, my lady?"

"I'm fine. I just have some work to do."

Paula made her way up the stairs, dragging her cumbersome limbs to her study. Lugging herself across the floor, she drooped at her desk and looked at all the parchments staring back at her. The girl's curly black locks stuck to her sweat lacquering her forehead, and her deprived blue eyes darted everywhere from the clock to a photo of her late family. The officers insisted she read the files for her own safety and insight; however, Paula knew the police had other reasons for her involvement. They saw her as a sort of fail-safe, a third person who could help their noble causes. The girl had seen it time and time again; a threat appears and the whole of society collapses, but miraculously, as soon as people from the upper classes got involved, society fixed themselves up. Just her luck to get wrapped in such affairs.

A familiar knock came at the door.

"Mistress, may I come in?"

"Enter."

The man came in cautiously, he had never known Paula to get enraged but she behaved as though she could lash at any moment. Paula buried her head in her hands. Thomas took this as an opportunity to scan the files at the desk.

"The police files for the ball, and"-

Thomas stopped himself from finishing his sentence. Paula lifted her head, running a hand through her fringe.

"I don't understand it, Thomas. They don't need my help but still"-

Thomas put a tender hand on her shoulder.

"You know as well as I that your support to this case is crucial. The public need a watchful eye, and the police need a sleuth."

"But I'm not a sleuth! I'm just me!"

The lady arose and ambled to the door.

"I'm going to take a stroll."

"My lady..."

Thomas failed to give a response in time, and so Paula walked past him and made her way to the manor's gardens.

"... You are not alone..."

The evening was rich with the smell of snowdrops and raw winter spices. The vast canvas above was painted in cool pastel colours, but a far-more ominous chill resonated from somewhere close by. All was quiet, a little too quiet for Paula's liking. In the setting dusk the trees looked savage, the bushes of ivory wove together like prison bars, no creature lay awake to notice her. Even the cloudy eye of the moon forbade an ounce of light to shine. In that moment, the girl wished she stayed under Thomas' watchful-

"MMH-"

A clammy hand tightened around her mouth and pulled her behind the manor's walls. Paula was held back against the bricks and couldn't turn to face her attacker.

"M-mercy..." she tried to beg but to no avail.

She could smell the alcohol dancing out of his mouth... the hot, toxic fumes hit the back of her neck hard. The stench of blood also lingered; it marked the criminal's skin like a tattoo. Just as she thought things couldn't spiral any further, a cold metal point skimmed the small of her back...

Chapter 10

A butler's oath

Thomas prodded the burning coal in the fireplace, the end of the iron poker bloomed an intense orange, making the flames flare and roar. The butler made sure the room was warm enough to keep out the night's chill. Clement brewed a pot of apple cider, whilst Christa filled the cushions with new cotton. When they found out the mistress was upset, they were ready to go above and beyond to lift her spirits.

"Erm, Thomas, why did the mistress run off anyway?"

Clement's question didn't sit well with the butler. Truth be told, Paula could have run off for a number of different reasons; the police bothering her, Audrey and Alister being in a state of peril, the horrid memories other's persisted making her recall.

"Well Clement"-

"Don't you remember Clement? Even when Mrs Ophelia first hired us, we witnessed the mistress' emotional fits." Christa interrupted Thomas, only making the butler more alarmed, and the chef more confused.

"Emotional fits? What do you mean?" said Thomas.

"It started after Paula's parents past away. She became bitter with mostly everyone and tended to conceal her emotions a fair bit."

"So, what you're saying is, even now she bares her burdens alone...?"

The woman nodded solemnly. Suddenly, the man felt a pain swell in his heart. Was he honestly so oblivious that he couldn't see how much the girl was hurting? At the ball she sat isolated from the rest of the party, in the manor she always wanted to read Jacob's book, and even with her precious butler, she hardly spoke when they travelled together. No matter how content she looked on the outside, that's how much her heart bled on the inside.

"I need to go find the mistress. It's been half an hour already."

The other two servants rushed at him when they noticed the heavy storm clouds forming through the window.

"You can't go alone mate, let me accompany you!"
With a hint of annoyance in his voice, Thomas blurted out his racing thoughts.

"Our mistress is out there, and I need you two to stay here just in case she comes back!"

Clement didn't seem to be as argumentative as he previously was, he sighed and turned away from the brunet man.

"You're right mate... go find Miss Paula."

The butler frowned a little but wasted no time heading out the front door. Thomas hoped he would find his mistress quickly and beat the overhead storm. To Thomas' growing misfortune, the family's carriage wasn't in its regular place, in fact, it was nowhere to be seen. That was odd, normally Cliffe was always so responsible. His house was only a short distance away from the manor, so failure to carry out his job was inexcusable. In that moment numerous questions fell upon the butler; but he had no time to be solving the case of the missing coach. The man continued to search the estate for a clue, a sign, anything that may help him locate Paula's whereabouts. Thomas scouted high and low but to no avail. The lady wasn't in the garden, nor was she in the greenhouse, or the field surrounding the estate. There was only one place she could be... London town.[7]

---

[7] The next few paragraphs of the book were in creation when the author was in secondary school.

*

The butler's cumbersome trudges and hoarse breathing was stifled by the flesh-numbing rain hailing from above. Thomas failed to decide whether it was his imagination or the light of the moon that caused London to look like a nightmare. Flying past all the sleeping houses and stalls, the butler found himself in the midst of a dark alley.

Even in his alcohol indulged days, the man never found himself in this part of town. Filthy water trickled down from the roofs above, tainting Thomas' refined uniform. The once pure white snow was now reduced to grey sludge; it slid down his shoes and fell into a flowing gutter beside his feet. Increasing his attention to the floor, the butler noticed the gutter stream stretched far beyond the alley, around a dimly lit corner. Call it what you will; instincts or a gut feeling, but Thomas had a compulsive urge to follow the water's current. After passing a shop selling ghoulish looking manikins, a roughish

---

She had a habit of creating the ends of her stories before the beginnings.

pub and an old pawn shop, the man stopped at a rundown factory.

A large, fractured pipe was hanging over the factory door. In between the gushing water and grime, was something else... it smelt a bit like iron. The man sniffed the air again and knew the water was polluted with blood. He had no choice but to break into the building. He was all about taking risks; this crimson life energy could belong to Paula.

Twisting the latch on the metal door, Thomas breathed a sigh of relief when it eventually edged open. A damp expansion of misplaced furniture and a flight of rotting stairs were standing before him. There wasn't much to explore on the ground floor except stain covered walls and broken household objects veiled in so much mould that some could categorise it as a fungus.

Noticing how fragile the railing really was, Thomas withdrew his shaking hand and steadied his footing against the stairs. He made sure each step's creak and moan were suppressed; the last thing he wanted was to give his position away. When the man reached the landing, only a lone door stood. Thomas softly pushed against the handle. It was locked from the inside. Squatting down and bearing his weight on his ankles, he peered through the keyhole.

There were all manner of sharp tools and materials scattered along the floor, including rope, dented knives, chairs, and rusted chains. There was a thin glass window to the back of the room, as well as a closed door on the right. In the centre of the room sat a beautiful young lady, she was tied to a chair with ropes biting at her ankles and wrists. She turned her head over to the door, as if feeling Thomas' presence-it was Paula. Even though she had a blindfold over her eyes and cloth around her mouth, it looked like she was begging her butler to save her.

"Mistress..."

Thomas was about to bash the door in, but then a click came from inside the room. The man frantically looked through the keyhole again, only to see none other than the Twisted Jester emerge from the other door.

The criminal's black and white Jesters mask was covered with specks of red and the cuffs of his long black cloak had stitching coming out of them. The Jester walked in delayed, anticipated strides, spiralling around Paula as if he were a wolf stalking a rabbit. Paula's head cocked left and right, trying to pin-point the tyrant's position. With a slow, somewhat seductive movement, the Jester undid Paula's blindfold and placed two gloved fingers under her chin. With visible disgust in her eyes, Paula flinched back and jolted her head to the left. Irritated by the girl's attitude, the Jester pulled back her hair until her muffled screams filled the room. He stared into her sapphire eyes, and for the first time Paula got a hard look at the masked figure's prominent green pupils.

As soon as Paula stopped struggling, the Jester released his grip and bent down to her thighs. Thomas' eyes felt hot with tears of anger, but as much as he wished to he couldn't intervene with the Jester so close to his mistress. The fiend took a weapon from his pocket and cut intricate designs into the girl's delicate skin. The dagger was the paintbrush, Paula was the canvas, and the Jester was about to create a bloody masterpiece if Thomas didn't act quickly. Grunting in a satisfied tone, the man stood up and put a finger to his lips, then he strode back into the other room.

Seizing what could be the only opportunity he would get; Thomas looked around for a useful object. Spotting a rusty pole leaning against the side of the staircase, he prodded it between the door and wall. With impeccable speed the man broke the latch, and rushed to his mistresses' side.

"Mmh"-

"Shh... mistress, I am going to get you out of here"-

Hearing the commotion, the Jester emerged from the other door again, dagger still in hand. The butler stood in front his mistress and pointed the pole's sharp end towards the Jester's chest. To the butler's astonishment, instead of lunging for him the Jester crept backwards.

"You bastard! Make your move!"

The butler inched closer to the murderer; each step he took made the Jester jolt back, until he was cornered against the wall. Thomas had the Jester in plain sight. He swung the pole with two hands; ready to decapitate him right there and then. Like lightning, the Jester seized a near-by chair and hurled it against Thomas' body! Thomas readied himself and caught the chair by the leg, one side ramming into his forearm. By the time he tossed the splintering chair to the side, the Jester's leather coat could be seen vanishing through the unlocked window.

Thomas stumbled to the window and scanned the sea of darkness below. The

Jester's quickened sprints could be heard against the puddles and cobblestones. The butler caught one last glimpse of the ends of his coat before he disappeared into an alleyway. It wasn't wise to go after him, especially since Paula was injured. As a faithful citizen it was Thomas' duty to catch the Jester, but as a butler it was his duty to safeguard his mistress. The man untied the gag around Paula's mouth, and cut the ropes restraining her with a shard of discarded glass. Taking off his tailcoat, Thomas draped the girl in the warm fabric, then delicately hoisted her up in his arms. Upon feeling his safe embrace, Paula leaned her head back onto his chest and gave a choked whisper-

"Thomas...I"-

Without letting her utter another word, Thomas placed an affectionate kiss upon her lips.

"Let's go home, my lady."

The two returned home, bruised, and weary. There was not a single carriage, coach, or horseman on the treacherous journey back home; Thomas needed to muster all his remaining strength to carry his mistress on foot.

*

Doctor Farthing arrived shortly after their return. Attire looking prim and proper, and a physician's bag in hand, he certainly looked far more professional than the doctor who took Alister in. The doctor bandaged Paula's thigh and ankles and prescribed her with herbal medicine, as well as plenty of bed rest. With one quick glance at his sleeping mistress, Thomas shut the door and turned to him.

"How is she looking, doctor?"

Still writing notes on a piece of paper, the doctor didn't look up while bestowing his best advice to the butler.

"Your mistress needs to have a good sleep. She has rope burns on her wrists and ankles, and has lost a bit of blood. Make sure you give her this..."

The doctor handed Thomas a bottle of medicine and the paper containing the timings to endorse it. Thomas took the medicine and slip of paper, then thought about the Jester's 'great' escape.

"Doctor, when should we report this incident to the police?"

Doctor Farthing placed his stethoscope and some splints in his bag before sighing.

"I will inform the authorities about the Jester's hideout, but for the sake of Lady Ethel's health, don't let the police interview her until she is well."

There was a slight tone of stringency in the man's voice, it's as if he knew something of Paula's injuries that Thomas did not.

"She might not be herself for a while. Do not hesitate to contact me if there are any persisting problems."

The butler shook hands with the man before stepping out the door and into the dreary night. No sooner than when the door shut did the other two servants appear from the kitchen. They came baring a tray of vegetable stew and hot tea.

"Me and Christa couldn't eat without you mate."

Thomas felt his chest prickle at the sentiment. It was astounding how a couple of months could turn colleagues into family. He gave a light-hearted smile and beckoned the two to come sit with him at the lounge table. They ate, they drank, not with a lot of conversation but more with a lingering, thoughtful silence. Thomas knew all too well that these small, bitter-sweet moments were fleeting. His mistress's life was threatened not once, but twice now, once at Miss Young's

ball and the second, tonight. Although he
had faith in the considerate gardener and
aloof chef, he feared that the Jester was far
too cunning, and one day all of their lives
would be in jeopardy.

-Tap tap tap-

There was a break in the peaceful moment.
Thomas was unsure if the others heard it, but
he could have sworn somebody tapped on
the front door...

"Wait here, I need to check
something."

The sudden change in Thomas' tone
caught the other servants off guard. They
were both used to the butler being cautious,
but when he grabbed the iron poker hanging
by the fireplace their faces drained to an ill-
white. Without explanation, the butler
stomped to the front room and rushed the
door. His itching fingers only lowered the
poker when he figured out who was quaking
in front of him.

"Mr Fulton, sir! What ya deein' lugging
that dangerous prodder arund...?"

It was Cliffe. He was standing, pale and soaked with rain. He fiddled with his soggy baker-boy hat, allowing the butler to inspect his drenched red hair. Behind him was the missing coach; not looking ransacked at all.

"Cliffe? What are you doing here at this time of night?"

The driver was about to speak his piece when suddenly he went into a fit of sneezing.

"You better come inside," said the butler.

Cliffe marked the floor with a trail of wet footprints, before sitting himself beside Clement.

"Mate, what happened to ya?" Clement asked.

"You should kna."

Clement was initially alarmed at the driver's harsh tone, but he brushed it off, remembering how moody he could get when he got caught in the rain. Thomas took a mental note of Cliffe's behaviour towards the chef, then urged the servants to make Cliffe feel welcomed.

"Christa, can you fetch a towel please, and Clement brew some tea would you."

The servants went to work while Thomas quizzed the man on the events that led up to his poor state. Cliffe explained that earlier in the evening someone came by his house and shouted to him from his front garden. They told him that Miss Paula was caught up with work at the north-end Teahouse and needed him to escort her back home. Without hesitation, Cliffe thanked the person standing outside and got ready for the long journey to the family business. But, when the driver finally arrived at the shop, the doors were locked and barred. He was frightened and thought Paula was either trapped inside the building or running around in the rain to get back home. With growing fear for Miss Paula's safety, Cliffe ran to the closest locksmith's shop, informed him of the situation, and opened the teashop. They both searched high and low, but Miss Paula wasn't anywhere. In all his wasted effort, he decided the best thing to do was to inform Thomas, and so, he came back to the manor.

When the driver finished his story, Thomas had a sickly expression on his face. He figured the time Cliffe was looking for Paula, was about the same time he was rescuing her from the Jester. That meant, it was no accident that the coach left as soon as Thomas needed it.

"Cliffe, listen carefully. Who was the person who told you Miss Paula was at the teahouse?"

The man's face fell slightly.

"From what I could tell... the person was too taal to be Christa, and they had a well-accented raspy voice..."

"Out with it, Cliffe!"

Giving a slight jump from hearing Thomas' severity, the driver gave his answer.

"I believe, it must have been Clement..."

Chapter 11

Burning the midnight oil

The butler was in utter disbelief when Cliffe blurted his response. Not only was he poking accusations at his fellow colleague, but he was also making a mockery of the Ethel servant's reputation. If Clement really were the one responsible for misleading Cliffe, that could only mean he knew Paula was going to be abducted, and that must mean he also knew Thomas was going to rescue her. Coming up with various theories, the butler wore his best poker face and cleared his throat.

"Was that all, Cliff?"
The red-haired lad nodded, still fiddling with the soggy hat sitting in his lap.

With impeccable timing the other two servants returned, bringing with them some towels and a pot of tea. The pair obliviously looked to Thomas; they had the feeling they had interrupted an important meeting or something of the sort. Eventually, Christa managed to hand Cliffe a towel. The driver gave the gardener a sweet smile. Clement didn't appreciate the gesture; he plopped the brew in front of him and gave an odd look.

Cliffe only scoffed at the tea like he was the world's snobbiest critic.

"Argh, that's it! Why are you acting like this, Cliffe? I thought we were mates?"

"We were mates, until you forced uz on a wild goose-chase!"

The chef's brows furrowed.

"Eh? I did no such thing!"

Cliffe stood from his seat.

"What a load of shi-"

"Cliffe!" The butler snapped.

The coachman cleared his throat and continued, "Earlier this evening you came by my hoose and towld uz Miss Paula needed to be picked up from the Tea Hoose."

"What!" Clement protested.

For most of the conversation Christa and Thomas didn't dare say a word, but the gardener knew that Clement was telling the truth.

"Cliffe, Clement couldn't have come to your house at that time because he was making apple cider."

Thinking carefully about their earlier schedule, Thomas agreed with Christa's statement. He distinctly remembered Clement brewing apple cider while he was tending to the fireplace.

"She's right, Cliffe. If we are talking about the same time, Clement couldn't have been at your house, because even I saw him in the manor's kitchen."

The driver sat back down in his chair. He wasn't prepared to believe Clement, but if the gardener and butler insisted it wasn't the chef, then how could he possibly go against all three of them? Thomas pondered further. If it wasn't Clement at Cliffe's house, who was it?

"Cliffe, what made you believe the person outside your home was Clement?" Thomas asked.

"Whey, I kna for sure it was a man. Ah could tell from his voice. And secondly, only you three, Miss Paula, Mrs Ophelia and Mr Finley kna where Ah live."

The room fell silent. The more they delved into this mystery, the more puzzling it became. Everyone shifted their gaze to each other. Not being able to decipher the truth was making their stomachs churn. Predictably, Thomas was the one who split the uncomfortable silence.

"Well, we can conclude a few things. The person outside Cliffe's house couldn't have been a woman, so that rules out the mistress, Christa, and Mrs Ophelia."

Thomas continued, "It couldn't have been myself or Clement either, because we were here at the manor, and Christa has evidence for that."

Clearly getting his confidence back, Clement spoke-up.

"That is true, but then the only person to blame would be Mr Finely, but he wouldn't do such a thing to his own family now, would he!"

The butler couldn't imagine Paula's grandfather tricking his servants, because, if that were true, it would also mean he wanted his own granddaughters' demise.

"I agree with you, Clement, I don't believe Mr Ethel would ever wish ill-will upon his family, let alone create a rift himself. No, I don't believe it was any of us at Cliffe's house..."

Suddenly, Cliffe's knuckles turned white against his navy hat.

"You can't really be suggesting...?"

"Yes. Whoever gave you false information was a third-party individual."

The whole room pondered, dwelled, and fretted into the early hours of the morning, but none of them could come up with a logical explanation. Growing more fatigued,

Cliffe got up to take his leave. Thanks to the fireplace his clothes were all dry and he was much warmer than when he arrived, but he was itching to get back to the comfort of his own home; he wasn't used to staying away from it. The chef and the gardener were also struggling to fight their heavy eyes; they saw Cliffe to the door, then retired to their quarters swiftly after. Thomas patted the driver's arm, but before he left the doorway, he enquired about something else that was troubling him...

"Cliffe, the chap outside your house... what was his attire?"
The driver looked back with an inquisitive eye.

"Whey, he was wearing a black flat cap and a grey overcoat, a similar outfit to the one Clement usually wears."

"Hmm..."

Thomas did recall the chef having that ensemble, but he still refused the thought of Clement conducting such a pitiful deed.

"What is it?" The driver asked.
Thomas lied and used the opportunity to pry even further.

"You are one of the Ethel servants, yet you live in a separate house. Why is that, Cliffe?"

Thomas could tell the question bothered him, but for once the butler didn't care. He was starting to get irked, the Ethel's had so many question marks in their history.

"Oh... it's just- Ah mean Ah did live with the other servants, years ago."

"Then, why not now?"
The driver's eyes glossed over.

"It was me parent's hoose and... Ah didn't want to leave it. Miss Paula knows what happened and she was gracious enough to let me live away from the estate."
Thomas started to understand. Cliffe was a special exception. Who were Cliffe's parents, the butler wondered?

"Mr Fulton?"

"Oh, apologies for all the questions, Cliffe. Make sure you reach home safely."

"Oh, erm, right you are, Mr Fulton."

The butler bowed as Cliffe left the manor. The man lingered in the driveway for a moment, wondering what revelations Thomas was brewing.

Leaning his back against the front door, Thomas wiped his brow with a handkerchief. If Cliffe was telling the truth, and the interloper who visited him really was wearing Clement's clothing, then the butler had to investigate something, something that if proven true, would change the severity of this mystery.

Thomas wandered the manor's empty halls, travelling past the living room, past the kitchen and the other servant's quarters, until he reached the back pantry. It wasn't much of an interesting place, just somewhere used to store footwear, umbrellas, and clothing for harsh weather[8]. When Thomas unlocked the door, he was both impressed and terrified to find his theory was correct. Everything from the shoes to the gloves were dry, however, Clement's overcoat and flat cap were damp... not only that, but the ends of the coat was splattered with crusting mud.

"Clement was indeed at the manor when the mystery man was busy misleading Cliffe, but he intentionally wore Clement's clothing to trick the driver into thinking he was the chef," Thomas mumbled to himself.

Slowly but surely, he was beginning to piece together this mystery.

The intruder at Cliffe's house mislead him on purpose. Somehow he knew Thomas

_____

[8] It might be helpful to refer to the Ethel manor floor plan to envision where Thomas was travelling.

would need the carriage to rescue the mistress. That could only mean the intruder snuck into the manor without anyone realising it.

The butler's blood ran cold. This fiend, this mastermind, he planned everything so articulately, it's as if he knew everyone's next move. He must have known Paula stormed off that night, he also must have known the servants were busy in the kitchen. That's the only time he could have snuck-in to steal the clothes!

Thomas returned to the living room, he grabbed the iron poker, double latched all the doors, and quickly peered into the other servants quarters. Clement and Christa were fast asleep and he was relieved to see one of them had took the liberty of reinforcing some of the windows. The man raced back upstairs and cautiously examined all the halls before stopping at his mistress' room. Taking a chair from the study, he propped it right outside Paula's door and sat there, guarding. He couldn't confirm his suspicion yet, but he wagered the Twisted Jester and the man who mislead Cliffe must be connected in some way. Tomorrow, the butler was going to conduct his own investigations, especially since Paula was unwell. Thomas prayed for strength to protect his mistress and he took those prayers to bed with him.

*

The next morning Paula awoke to the aroma of sausages and egg. She rubbed her eyes and let out a pained squeak as an ache throbbed in her thigh. All at once the horrifying memories of yesterday flooded her mind. When the Jester caught hold of her in the garden, she began to struggle against him. The Jester fought with her for some time before she fell unconscious. The next thing she knew she was tied to a chair in a dingy, unfamiliar room. The Jester toyed with her, cut her with daggers and gripped her flesh so tightly it caused a trail of bruises to erupt on her skin. Paula turned over her arms and examined all the unique wounds, some of them where bandaged, others were purple and scabbing.

"Mistress...?"

Paula dragged the tips of her fingers over her forearm, then over her neck. She turned her head left and right, examining every new mark bore onto her body. It didn't matter that the mirror was at the end of the room; she could clearly see the vivid plum bruises in her reflection.

"Come now, mistress. After you eat, I can give you some medicine."

Gradually, the girl let her hands fall back onto the duvet. Her coiled fringe veiled her eyes, and a single tear ran down her cheek. Thomas felt a prickling in his tired green eyes, he kneeled at his mistress' side and wrapped his arms around her body. In between shedding tears, he whispered sweet sentiments to her; comforting words and heartfelt thoughts. They both stopped weeping after that, and Thomas took the liberty of feeding the girl breakfast. On her own the girl wouldn't eat, but when her butler was so considerately popping spoonsful of egg, sausage, and beans in her mouth, she couldn't refuse. The girl hadn't eaten well since the incident, so when her plate was near-empty, Thomas couldn't be more pleased. He also gave the girl a dose of the herbal medicine; she took it quite well and hauled down the whole spoonful.

"Mistress, go back to sleep now. I'll be back before dinnertime."

"Where are you going, Thomas?"

Thomas suddenly smiled. His mistress actually spoke! He was beginning to worry that he may never hear that angelic voice of hers again.

"I'm going to deliver the drawing to Bridgedale and see if I can find anything out."

"But Thomas"-

The butler stroked the girl's silky hair and placed a strand behind her ear.

"But nothing, my lady, you are in no condition to be running around. Please rest, Christa and Clement will be here to take care of you a while."

Paula dropped her gaze.

"Well, alright, but promise me you'll be careful."

"I promise," Thomas said.

The man tucked the blanket over Paula, then took Alister's drawing from the desk and folded it into his pocket. The man then took the breakfast tray from the nightstand, went to the door and looked at his mistress again.

"Pleasant dreams, mistress..."

In the Kitchen, Clement was anxiously pacing up and down. Christa only followed his movements with her eyes, leisurely sipping on her rose tea.

"What if the mistress doesn't eat breakfast! Aw, she ain't gonna get better

unless she eats quick!" The brunet man
stammered.

"Are you forgetting who the mistress is
with? Thomas is the best butler this house
has ever seen. He will get her to eat for sure,"
the gardener replied.

"Are you two quite alright?"
Thomas entered the kitchen, balancing a
bunch of utensils and cutlery in hand.

"Thomas! Mate, did the mistress eat
her breakfast?"

The butler couldn't help but chuckle,
it was always reassuring to know that the
other servants cared for Paula so dearly. It
was easier for him to part with Paula knowing
that Clement and Christa were never too far
away.

"Yes, indeed Clement, the mistress has
eaten her breakfast and is having a nap now."

The chef breathed a sigh of relief, and
finally sat down in front of his cold tea.
Thomas lit up the stove and started to brew a
new pot for him.

"You don't need to do that mate."

"Nonsense, I can't let you drink cold
tea now, can I?"

For the first time, Christa noticed how
close Clement and Thomas were. It amazed
the gardener that Clement opened up to

someone so quickly, the only other person he instantly got along with was Paula. Suddenly, she remembered how demure Morris used to be, especially when they were first acquainted. The blonde was elated to know the man had someone else to rely on besides herself.

"Well you two, I have a few errands to run, but I should be back before evening. Take care of the mistress for me."

The two servants didn't ask the butler what errands he was going to conduct. Their only concern was to ensure Paula's' health and wellbeing.

"Don't fret mate, we'll do a right good job taking care of the mistress."

Thomas smiled and placed a hot cup of tea on the table. While the two servants were occupied with breakfast, the butler made haste. He slid on his black overcoat and tightened a red scarf around his neck, before emerging into the winterland waiting for him. Thomas informed Cliffe about his departure a few minutes after putting the mistress to sleep, he shouldn't be too far away now.

In the distance, Thomas could hear the turning wheels of the coach and the horse's clopping hooves. The man adjusted his gloves and walked to the side of the driveway.

"Ah hope am not late!" Cliffe called out from the driver's seat.

"Not at all, you're right on time, Cliffe."

Thomas waited for the horses to halt, then climbed into the carriage and anticipated the sound of the whipping reins. Sure enough the sound came along with the follow-up of neighs and once again the carriage was off to London town.

The journey was one of near-silence since Thomas couldn't talk to Cliffe, who was on the carriage's outer seat and of course, Paula wasn't here either. On several occasions however, Thomas instinctively looked over to his left, as if waiting for Paula to magically appear. It seemed like this quiet was lonelier than the normal comfortable silence the man was used to.

After the considerably long and eventless ride, Cliffe dropped Thomas outside a little shop. All sorts of clocks and antiques were displayed in the glass window, Thomas could hear them ticking faintly. A large, wooden sign hung above the building, labelled '*Bridgedale, masters of antiques.*'

"Thank you Cliffe, I won't be too long."

"Nee bother, Mr Fulton."

Cliffe tied the horse's reins to a lamppost at the side of the pavement then began reading a crumpled newspaper from his pocket.

Thomas entered the quaint looking shop to the sound of a bell. He was immediately overwhelmed with the smell of candle wax and newly cut wood; surprisingly, it was a pleasant scent. There were all manner of clocks hanging off the walls; intricate wooden timers, monochrome-coloured watches, even a great grandfather clock standing against the back wall. There were cases filled with delicate china, marble statues, and exotic brooches, Thomas was particularly allured to a beautifully cut ring, dainty and etched in gold. After briefly investigating the shop's various goods, Thomas ventured to the front counter where a bookish looking man was rotating various cogs into a cracked clock.

"Tom he was a piper's son, he learned to play when he was young..."[9]

Beside the keeper, slouching on a stool, was a little blonde girl wearing a long sky-blue dress. She was fiddling with the silver crank of a music box and sang along to the traditional tune that played. As Thomas got closer to the desk, her singing became quieter and her wistful smile evolved into a shy one. The man behind the counter noticed the girl had halted her singing and looked up from his workstation.

"How may I help you, good sir?" The keeper beamed.

Thomas wore his best smile while addressing the man; he didn't want to give too much information away regarding the real reason he was there.

"Good day, I was wondering if you could tell me what kind of pocket watch this is."

The butler unfolded the drawing and handed it to the man. He adjusted his glasses, and slightly squinted as he dug the paper in his face.

---

[9] The nursery rhyme *Tom Pipers son* is a very crucial part of the book. Not only does it fit the tone of the writing, but Tom is also the nickname of Thomas.

"Hmm, well this looks like one of the custom-made pocket watches we used to manufacture a while back."
The man set the drawing on the table and began to observe it from afar.
"Custom made you say?" Said Thomas.
"Why yes, many antique connoisseurs came from all over London to get a watch tailored to their specific requirements."
Trying to sound less interrogative and more genuine, Thomas put on a curious tone and enquired further about the custom watches. He sounded like a little boy asking his father why the sky was blue or some other innocent question like that.
"What makes this watch custom made?
"Well, the circular border around the edge is fashioned into miniature rectangles and there are initials written on the lid."
On the outside the butler only grinned and nodded, but on the inside, he was brainstorming hundreds of theories.
"I see, when did you say you sold these watches?" Thomas said.
"Erm, I would say about fifteen years ago."

Fifteen years? That was a substantial amount of time for a pocket watch to be preserved so well, especially considering it needed to be in a good state for Alister to draw it from memory.

"Well, thank you for being such a help. I was actually interested in buying a watch that looked like this one."
The shop owner chortled.

"I'm afraid we don't sell ones like this any more, but I do have something that might pique your curiosity..."

After a few minutes Thomas emerged out of the shop with a small paper bag. The man sold him a silver pocket watch with a golden boarder and platinum Roman numerals. Apparently, it was the last of his 'gold-graced collection' and was a great value for money. Truth be told, the butler only brought it so he wouldn't seem obnoxious. It was vexing to go through all this trouble, but the man managed to gather some crucial information. There was something else he ended up buying, though he wasn't sure at what point he'd gift it to his mistress.

The journey back was full of anticipation; Thomas couldn't even breathe properly until he reached the manor's glistening gates. When the carriage pulled up in the front yard, and the wheels were once again familiar with the brittle gravel below, Thomas hopped out the backseat, paper bag in hand.

"Thank you, Cliffe."

Cliffe tipped his hat, "Happy to help, Mr Fulton!"

Cliffe directed the horses back on the main road, no doubt the driver was going to take a well-deserved rest, or procrastinate in the comfort of his own home. Thomas lingered outside for a moment, and admired the snow covering the roof and brickwork. He didn't know why, but it was oddly calming to observe the light snow falling from the darkening sky above. The butler opened the door to the manor and the other two servants rushed him as soon as he set foot inside.

"Thomas! The mistress has been asking for you for ages!" Clement shouted.

Upon hearing this, the butler ripped off his scarf and coat and ran upstairs without any further details. Clement looked rattled but Christa only had a smirk on her lips.

"Don't fret Clement, the mistress will be just fine now."

Thomas sprinted over each step and glided across the hallway. When he reached his mistresses' room, he noticed the doorknob was jittering. He put his own hand on the door and whispered...

"My lady...?"

There was a mumble from the other side, and a small, pale face looked up at him.

"Thomas, you were gone for too long..."

The man let out an elongated sigh and hugged the wide-eyed girl. Out of all the people Thomas met, Paula was the only one who made him truly worry. It may seem selfish of him, but the connection he shared with *his* lady ran deeper than anyone else's. The man let his hands feel her forehead and the wounds on her arms. She didn't have a temperature, and the cuts were no longer sore.

"I'm sorry I was away for so long, but I came back before dinner, just like I promised."

"That doesn't matter, I'm not hungry anyway," said Paula.

The lady frowned as she ran her fingers through her hair.

"Honestly, the other servants are incompetent when it comes to fixing a proper bath."

Unexpectedly, the butler started chuckling.

"Is that why you missed me? You wanted me to run you a bath?"

"Stop laughing, it isn't at all amusing!" Struggling with his laughter, Thomas waved his hands dismissively and walked towards the bathroom.

"As you wish mistress, I'll run a 'proper' bath for you."

Instantly, a satisfied smile crossed Paula's features. She did indeed care for all her servants, but never had she had such a deep connection like the one she shared with Thomas. The girl sat at the edge of her bed and swung her feet from side-to-side. She wasn't sure why she was feeling so jovial, but she had to admit it felt good not having to dwell on the past. No matter what she looked at, no matter what she thought about, only the image of Thomas entered her mind.

"Your bath is ready, my lady."

Thomas bowed and ushered his mistress to the bathroom door. When the lady passed him, she suddenly grabbed hold of his hand and smiled.

"Stay with me, won't you Thomas?"

The man's cheeks flushed bright pink; did Paula really just ask him to stay with her while she bathes? He coughed and looked around the room. It's true, one of a butler's many duties was to bathe his master, but Paula had never asked him to do such a thing in the months prior, so why now he wondered.

"If that's what you wish, my lady."

Paula walked with such elegance as she entered the bathroom, every so often she cast a smirk over her shoulder. Thomas gulped, he had never seen his mistress act in such a way, could it be she was coming down with a fever of some sort? Without any warning, she undid her nightgown and let it drop to the floor, Thomas looked away swiftly, the memories of Paula's words fresh in his mind. A couple of months ago all she repeated was: 'Thomas close your eyes!' but now she was behaving like a charming temptress. With never-faltering poise she dipped her body in the water and called to the blushing butler.

"Do you mind putting soap in my hair?"

Thomas opened one eye, his lady was shrouded in bubbles, and only the top of her chest and head were visible. Feeling a little less tense, the butler went over and rubbed some soap into his hands. If he got this over with quickly, Paula might not notice his flushed face. The girl's hair was silky, her neck was quite soft too... what was Thomas thinking! He shook his head and tipped a jug of warm water over her.

"Don't you adore how heated water can be, Thomas?"

The man gulped. He could sense the deeper meaning behind his mistress's words. Just like water Paula's affections could run cold... or heat up. While thinking about the intentions of his mistress's capricious behaviour, he eyed the back of her bare body and shivered.

She soaped up her arms and chest. Thomas gulped. The girl's lips formed into a smirk as she held out her arms, waiting for him. Thomas propped forward and poured another jug of water on her.

"All done, mistress."

She tucked back her fringe, "Take me out, would you?"

The lady continued to stare at her butler nonchalantly, even when his own eyes flickered in embarrassment.

"As you wish."

Thomas unfolded a newly ironed towel and covered up the girl so quickly so he couldn't catch a glimpse of her bare skin, then he hoisted her up and carried her to the bedroom. The butler propped Paula down by the bed and hurried to the wardrobe. The faster she was put to bed; the faster Thomas could stop thinking about ludicrous things. When he turned back around, the damp towel was on the floor, Paula was sitting on the bed with her knees tucked close to her chest. The butler couldn't turn away, not this time, he couldn't think of a word to say either. Never did he imagine his mistress was this beautiful.

"You're probably wondering why I'm acting so strangely."

Thomas was astounded; it was as if Paula read his mind! He inched closer to her and looked straight into her eyes.

"When I was being held captive, the only person I could think about was you. At some point I started to think I was going to die. I couldn't bear the thought of not seeing you again, not being able to hear your voice again..."

The girl paused, and looked at the silky sheets slipping between her fingers.

"I just want to make the most of this moment. Who knows how long we'll have it for?"

The man fell to his mistresses' side and embraced her tightly. His embarrassment now washed away with regret.

"I love you, my lady. Please don't shed another tear."

Paula looked up as Thomas took her hand in his.

"I have something I want to gift you." Thomas took a little purple and gold ring from his pocket.

"I saw it at Bridgedale and I just had to."

He watched a blush form on Paula's cheeks and waited for her reaction.

"Oh, Tom..."

Thomas felt his chest tighten. That was the first time his mistress had called him by his pet name. She held out her finger and waited for him.

"P-Paula..." he stuttered.

The lady giggled a little in return

"I've always known it was you."

There was a warm silence as Thomas slid the ring on his lady's finger.

"It's a beautiful ring," she said.

"Not as beautiful as you, my lady."

The man kissed the back of Paula's hand. She leaned in closer, smiling with emotions Thomas hadn't seen in her before. He pecked her forehead, her cheek, her lips, until he finally made his way to her neck. She tangled her arms around his back and dug her face into his chest. The butler only realised it now that he was so close to her but-Paula was so petite, and fragile looking... he was afraid one touch would break the lady. He prudently ran his hands up and down her body. She was warming-up. Paula looked away for an instant, then closed the distance between their panting mouths.

"I love you too, Thomas."

Many emotions coursing through him, Thomas let his warmth encase Paula.

"Oh, Paula..."

In between blissful tears the girl graced her butler's ears with soft moans. Through the thin veil of the curtain, the full moon's silvery light flooded the room, illuminating the silhouettes of a lady and her butler...

Chapter 12

Truth hurts

The door to the library was left ajar. Thomas sat by a burned-out candle, scribbling notes on a scrap of parchment. With Alister's drawing to the right of him, he referred to all the markings and symbols, frantically trying to make a connection with the information he gathered from Bridgdale.

Thomas concluded the morning meal service and put the mistress back to bed, after that, all he had been doing was investigating the case of the pocket watch. He was especially motivated since Paula admitted her true feelings to him the previous night; she was afraid of losing her butler to the hands of the Jester and wanted nothing more than to stay in Thomas' arms. The butler couldn't help but think the pocket watch was significant to this case, however, he didn't care either way. If catching the Jester would aid his mistress, then he would do anything and everything in his power to put him behind bars.

The man working at Bridgedale mentioned something about initials... when

Thomas examined the drawing again, he did notice three squiggly lines on the lid of the watch, but it was quite hard to decipher. After a while lost in thought, the butler concluded that the only letters that resembled the squiggly lines were the letters *I, L, T, J* or *F.* There were only three lines. That meant whoever owned this watch had three initials. Of course, it was a possibility that the chap at Bridgedale was mistaken. Maybe they weren't initials at all, maybe they were a code for something?

"Hmm... deciphering this was more of a challenge than I thought."

Thomas' words trailed off into the vast quiet of the dimly lit room. He tucked Alister's drawing and the hastily written notes into any old book and carried it away to his room. The man had only been absent from his room for one night, but the air was already ice cold.

Thomas threw the book in his bedside draw then caught sight of the window; it was snowing viciously. It saddened him, not being able to see the energising rays of the sun, or the great wall of garden hedges.
'*Better check on those two,*' he thought to himself as he roamed into the stairway.

Last time the butler checked, Clement was reading an impressive recipe book, and Christa was sweeping the front room. When Thomas reached the bottom of the stairs he was greeted with silence. The front room was spotless, and a freshly baked strawberry shortcake was placed on the kitchen counter. Well, at least the other servants were staying on top of their chores.

"Clement! Christa!"

Opening the door to the living room, Thomas found the two servants looking over the lounge table. They didn't look up, or even respond to Thomas calling their names. The man ambled towards them and caught a glimpse of what they were so fixated with, it was the morning paper.

'Jester's hideout found!

In the filthiest ends of London town, it was discovered the infamous Twisted Jester had been seeking refuge in the midst of an old factory! Instruments of torture, from daggers to scalpels were found in a secret upstairs room; it leaves us all to wonder... who is their next victim, and where will they strike next?'

The butler had only skim-read the first few lines and a sickly dread began forming in the pit of his stomach. The police had broken into the room that the Twisted Jester kept running into that night, no doubt they must have found something gruesome. Thomas couldn't bear to keep reading. As if Christa heard the man's thoughts, she spoke up.

"The police found several diagrams of nobles and a stash of books containing risky medical operations."
The hairs on the back of the man's neck stood on edge... *diagrams of nobles?*

"Does it say which nobles were targeted?" The butler held his breath.

"No," Christa replied bluntly.

Thomas ran a hand through his hair in frustration. He began to think, and sure enough it came to him. That day when Doctor Farthing arrived to see Paula, he said the authorities would pay them a visit once she was in a state to answer questions. Now that the news was in the papers, the butler was sure the police would come sooner than expected. It was right to assume that the officers would also inform them on the diagram of nobles, well, only if it concerned Paula of course. Acknowledging that the other servants were studying him intently, the man adjusted his tie and took out his pocket watch.

"Right, enough lollygagging. Our lady needs us to be strong, as servants we must carry out our obligation, so let us continue with the day."

Clement and Christa looked at each other, half with fear, half with admiration.

"Clement, if you would kindly start with lunch. Christa, would you help me clean the parlour, please?"

They both nodded, and went off to work. With new-found motivation, Clement took out his recipe book and flicked to the page depicting a beef casserole. Christa followed Thomas to the parlour and eyed a bit of string hanging loose from one of the sofa cushions. She glanced over to Thomas who was shaking his head at the burned-out fireplace, which was spewing out bits of ash and dust. Thomas already had his hands full, so the gardener didn't bother asking if she should sew the pillows back up. As the butler rolled up his sleeves, and delved into the lumps of crumbling coal, Christa took out a sewing kit from the towering glass cupboard in the corner of the room.

Taking out a cherry-coloured thread, she propped it through a small needle and started to stitch the cushion in small loops. Even though her body was in the parlour, her mind was wondering elsewhere; she couldn't help but think it was her that was meant to be abducted that day. Christa knew she was a calm minded person, but also very stubborn. That day she ran off to the greenhouse, it could have been her who got kidnapped, but it didn't play out that way. Why was it that Paula had to be the one who got taken, why wasn't she there to protect her? Christa fell back into reality as she prodded her finger with the needle's sharp point. A spec of blood pooled at the tip of her finger. She let it bleed out, staring at it. Thomas turned his head and looked at the girl's dwindling expression.

"Christa! You're bleeding!"
The woman smiled a strange smile and took out a handkerchief from her pocket.

"I'm fine," she wiped away the blood and smiled again.

The butler could tell the difference between a liar and a saint, and he wasn't at all convinced with Christa's reaction.

"Don't lie, I can tell something is bothering you."
Contemplating her next words, Christa lifted her head to meet the butler.

186

"I'm just disappointed in myself, I failed to protect the mistress. I'm so unbelievably stubborn... I can't even comprehend the consequences of my actions."

Tears stinging her eyes, the girl had a sudden recollection of her sister. As the second born child, Christa didn't get as much attention as her precious sister Gloria did. In all honesty, she was envious of her, and on many occasions threw tantrums about the pettiest of things, all in hopes of getting attention. But no matter how resentful she acted; Gloria loved her all the same. In fact, she bestowed her with more courtesy than her parents ever did. Even back then Christa never thought about consequences, and one day her fault became her sister's punishment.

After losing what she treasured most, Christa stumbled upon Ophelia who offered her a job she couldn't refuse. Again, Christa took the opportunity out of selfishness, but then her eyes met Paula's. There was sincerity in the girl's pupils, she cared for Christa out of the goodness of her heart, not for reputation or gain. Something in Paula reminded the girl of her sister, and from then on, she promised to work not in self-interest but for the good of all around her.

"Christa," Thomas spoke softly, "we can't stop the inevitable, but we can strive to make the best out of it."

The woman went quiet. She understood what Thomas meant. Yes, Paula did get hurt, but at least she was still here.

"What's with all the frightful faces?"

Paula stood in the doorway with a beaming smile. Thomas and Christa immediately ran to support her, but the girl simply lifted a hand.

"Don't worry, I'm feeling much better now."

The two servants cracked a smile, it was a relief to see Paula back on her feet. As if right on cue, Clement rang the bell for lunch. The three of them ventured to the dining room, where plates of casserole were laid out neatly on the table. Clement pressed his back against the kitchen door, and emerged into the room with a basket full of fresh bread. He almost lost his balance when he saw Paula standing in between the other servants.

"Mistress! It's nice to see you back down here!"

"It's wonderful to be back, Clement."

Suddenly his smile faded. He looked between the basket of bread and the dining table.

"I'm sorry my lady, I didn't think you would be coming down, so I set the table for us lot. We could eat in the kitchen and leave you be if you wish."

"Don't be silly, Clement. I think we should all eat together for a change."

Since Paula declared it, the others weren't going to try and sway her mind, especially since they were all so ravenous. The fragrance of stewed carrots and lean beef lingered around the table. Paula could also smell the sweetness of caramelised onions and parsnips. The food tasted better than it smelled, the crispiness of the battered potatoes, the light aftertaste in the dressed salad. Even the saltiness of the gravy made everyone lick their lips. After the meal was devoured, the chef brought out the strawberry shortcake, which Thomas noticed had been coated with a light dusting of icing sugar (no doubt to satisfy Paula's sweet tooth).

"That was delicious, thank you Clement."

"Aww, think nothin' of it, my lady."

Beholding all the smiles and satisfied faces, Thomas didn't want to break the cheerful atmosphere, but he needed to tell Paula about the news, and how the authorities would be coming to interview her. Christa nudged Clement and mouthed for him to step into the Kitchen. They took the dishes from the table then left the two alone in the dining room. The butler walked in the next room and pulled out Paula's chair, directing her to take a seat.

"Mistress, I'm delighted that you are feeling well, and I'm sorry to be the bearer of bad news but this was issued this morning."

Thomas handed the girl the newspaper and watched as her eyes jumped from line-to-line. Gradually, her hold on the newspaper tightened. She gripped it to the point where Thomas could hear the corners of it crumple. With a sluggish movement, she put the newspaper down on the table and sighed.

"If this news has reached the public, doesn't that mean I will be interviewed soon?"

Thomas nodded; he was glad his mistress caught onto things so quickly.

"Well in that case, we should sit tight and wait. I'm sure they would be arriving sooner than we think."

"Of course, mistress."

Paula took out a book from the side of the arm-chair, (Thomas hadn't noticed it was there earlier). '*That day in autumn*' he thought to himself. Thomas began to wonder how many times Paula must have read that book. It was as if she was expecting a different outcome or something of the sort. The butler knew all too well that stories were just stories and that fate never changed.

*

Just as the two predicted, the authorities arrived later that evening to enquire about Paula's kidnapping. To their surprise it was the same two policemen who graced them the day they returned from Audrey's manor.

"Good evening, Miss Paula," the taller, white-haired officer said.

"Good evening," She replied cautiously.

Thomas pulled out chairs for the two men, then took a seat next to his mistress. It was different this time, the officers permitted Thomas to stay as he also came into contact with the Jester. The butler was pleased about this. He doubled down on the thought, leaving his mistress alone was something he despised. The other, shorter officer, who had a scar on his right cheek, clutched a bunch of papers in his hands. Thomas looked at him, but he only gave a blank stare in return.

"Right, let's get straight down to business," the tall officer said.

"As you may have seen in the papers, we investigated the Jester's hideout to find a diagram depicting various members of the nobility. Amongst them were Viscount Landers, Earl Randal, Baron Keith, Duke Knox, and some others with crosses painted over their photographs."

A slight pang hit the butler's chest, as he heard his late master's name. But within an instant he was intently listening to the officers again.

"There were other Nobles photographs on the diagram that were circled in red, including Miss Young, Earl Archie Stitch, and yourself, Miss Paula."

The girl's heart began to beat faster as she remembered the Jester's sturdy hold around her mouth. If Thomas hadn't rescued her, where would she be now?

"Now, in light of this evidence, two officers will be patrolling Miss Young, Earl Stitch, and your estate to ensure your safety."

Thomas and Paula simultaneously breathed a sigh of relief as the officers finished their explanation. The other, cold-sounding officer finally spoke out loud.

"We've told you what we know, now we need you to answer some questions. When you were being held captive, did the Jester say anything to you?"

"No," Paula replied.

"Alright. Did the Jester take off his mask, or could you describe any distinctive features?"

"Well, I couldn't see anything of his face except his narrow, dark-green eyes."

The officer scribbled something down on the report then looked back up to Paula.

"How did the Jester escape that day?"

"He jumped out of the window," Thomas stated.

Paula concurred with Thomas' statement and the officer's quills began scribbling away again.

"Which way did he run?"

Thomas thought hard, "An alley which was near a pawn shop and a pub... the *old leather bottle*[10] or something like that."

The officers nodded, "Thank you for your co-operation, that will be all."

Thomas and Paula both looked puzzled. The officers only came by to ask them a few questions? Before either of them could inquire further, the officer with the scar spoke again.

"Doctor Farthing explained details about your injuries. I'd imagine you don't want to recall them, Miss Paula."

The girl nodded. The light-haired officer stepped in with a friendly smile and a reassuring look in his eyes.

"Very well then, we'll be off to deliver this information to the station, then we will send some officers to guard your manor."

"Thank you, sirs," Paula replied.

Both of the men tipped their hats as they walked back outside to their coach. Thomas immediately closed the door; the fear of the Jester's cruelty sinking into his

---

[10] The Old Leather Bottle pub mentioned in the story was inspired by a real life pub which was founded in the 16th century.

mind. Paula rested a hand on her butler's arm and smiled fondly.

"Don't fret Thomas, soon the Jester will be caught and everything will be alright, you'll see."

Paula turned herself towards the stairs, but didn't move further until casting another look at her butler.

"I'm going to continue with my reading. Please bring my evening tea to the study at the usual time."

The butler watched his mistress leave and looked to the newly stitched crimson cushions. Somehow, he felt a sense of deja-vu.

Thomas made his way into the kitchen where Clement was washing dishes and Christa was drying them. They smiled when he entered, but Thomas could tell from their eyes that they were frightened too. Whether it was fear for the mistress's safety, or fear of the Jester's ruthlessness-he couldn't tell. While the servants were occupied, Thomas took out a monochrome checked case from under the kitchen table and unclipped the gold hinges.

"A game of chess anyone?" Thomas asked with a raised eyebrow.

Both servants observed each other then cracked into a grin.

"Ha, only if Morris wants to lose again!"

The chef slammed the tea towel down by the sink and turned around dramatically.

"No way will I loose now, Wood. Thomas taught me the ins and outs of this game!" Clement winked.

Soon enough the three companions were huddled around the kitchen table, dodging rooks, jumping past pawns, and eyeing each other's king. Thomas played the mercenary, ready to help both sides if they really needed it. The butler had to admit he was impressed, both the gardener and the chef played with such skill, he'd wager they wouldn't do too badly in a professional match. After an hour of strategical game playing, Clement emerged the victor, winning six matches out of ten.

"Didn't I tell you I would win, mate!" Clement began to gloat, while Christa folded her arms and pouted.

"You could be a little more gracious about it you know, I played the game well too."

The chef halted his shenanigans, and leaned his elbows on the table.

"You're right Christa; you play the game well... I just play it better!"

Clement started laughing again but not for long. The blonde girl leaped up and grabbed a hold of his ear. In between his yelps and pleas, Thomas heard a knock at the front door...

"Excuse me," The butler left the other servants to their own devices and went to the door.

The man looked through the window, making out two figures in uniform. Ah, the officers had arrived. The two men looked strangely timid for officers of the law, but Thomas was in no-place to judge. The butler was courteous, but he still couldn't understand why these two were the ones chosen to patrol the manor.

The officers told the man they would be patrolling every few hours, making rounds until sunrise. Thomas couldn't imagine it would be very comfortable seeking refuge in a carriage only to walk back out into the cold afterwards, but he supposed it was their duty as protectors of the country. As Thomas shut out the night's chill, he realised the time! He only had fifteen minutes to brew Paula's evening tea. Thomas ambled back into the kitchen where Clement and Christa were still squabbling.

"Sorry to cut your antics short, but I need to prepare the mistress' evening tea."

Once the two stopped behaving like unsupervised children in a playground, they began to help Thomas by finding the mistresses' favourite China tea set and generously plating the tray with Marie biscuits. Thomas reckoned Paula would fancy earl grey today, since she hadn't had it in a while. The man began to imagine the great smile on Paula's face when she'd take a bite of the sweet treats, she was indeed very adorable when she enjoyed her food. The whistle of the teapot brought Thomas out of his daydreams. He generously plated the biscuits and tea on a tray and travelled to the stairs. The butler could hear the wind howling from above, it was probably still snowing too. A sudden shiver travelled down his spine and he thought about how he must get the fireplace ready in Paula's room.

As he reached the landing and made his way down the hall, he felt an unexplainable sensation telling him to move faster...

Without dawdling, Thomas ran to the study and didn't waste time knocking on the door. He swung the door open and came just in time to see a masked figure standing at the window.

"Mistress! Watch out!"

Paula, who was so engrossed in her book, spun her head around just before the Jester lashed at her with a sharpened dagger. When the figure saw Thomas drop the tray and charge at him, he pulled his usual stunt of jumping out the window, but this time, Thomas wasn't having it. The butler skid across the floor, and hoisted himself up onto the windowpane. The Jester was using the ivy to climb back to the ground. If the Jester could do it, so could Thomas. The man grabbed a hold of the sturdy vines and let himself descend with ease. When he reached the snow-covered driveway, he spun around to see the Jester bolting out of the manor's gates.

Thomas couldn't think clearly any more. All he knew was the Jester was a threat to his mistress and therefore a threat to him. The butler ran after him like a loyal dog chasing a mangy cat. Along the side of the pavement, Thomas saw the fresh bodies of two officers in the snow. Their blood smeared the white frost like something out of a horror novel. The butler grit his teeth as he ran past them, his aching legs picking up speed. The Jester was heading for London town-the south side. Thomas continued to run after him, even though the discomfort of the cold was settling in. The snow was just below his knees, and fresh flakes still fell from above. It was becoming increasingly difficult to see anything, but the butler didn't give up.

Stumbling through the ocean of snow, the man finally saw the Jester ahead of him.

"There's nowhere to run, Jester!"

Thomas cornered the masked murderer against the newly built Stone-Arch bridge. There was nothing to do except fight. The Jester brought out his dagger and lifted it right above his head. He struck fast, and tore right into Thomas' tailcoat! For a moment, the weapon was stuck. Thomas kicked the Jester in the face, causing the dagger to disappear into the piles of snow. Back pressed against the bridge, the Jester felt the icy bricks through his gloved hands. Thomas jerked forward, and gripped the Jester's collars.

"It's over, you bastard!"

The Jester cackled as Thomas' grip tightened around his neck. He moved his hand, not in urgency or terror. The Jester moved his hand slowly, lifting the mask from his face...

"*From what you become... you cannot run...*"

The butler's pupils broadened as he took in the features of the man behind the mask. With a sudden movement, the Jester leaned back against the bridge, making Thomas' hold on him falter. The villainous man seemed to fall in a dreary slow motion as he descended from the bridge and into the freezing river below.

The butler was frozen in place; shock and disbelief painted on his features. He dropped to his knees and stared dumbly at the spot where the Jester was previously standing. In the distance, the sound of hurrying hooves echoed closer and closer.

Chapter 13

A path is carved

Jacob Lester Lockhart, 21 years old, Profession: butler. The highly intellectual and at times, prideful man, was born into a middle class family. The Lockhart's were well known for their great minds of literature and psychology, and these talents were apparent in Jacob from a very young age. His love of books grew from fairy tales and fiction to mystery and medical studies, and soon enough he began to write his own novels. It was a struggle at first; he couldn't seem to find the right inspiration for his writings, and so his parents managed to enrol him for a university scholarship. The change was beneficial for the young lad. The work wasn't too strenuous, and the environment was just as inspiring as he imagined. Just when Jacob thought life couldn't get any sweeter, he met her...

Lady Evelyn Moore was an independent, charming young lady who was the daughter of a very famous businessman. Through whispers and rumours, Jacob found out that Miss Evelyn was studying business and was preparing herself to take over her father's jewellery company. Well, that was to be expected since she was an only child.

Jacob wasn't really the coy type, actually he was quite the opposite; young girls and older women alike swooned over his porcelain-like features and natural gentlemanly flare. One day he waltzed right up to Miss Evelyn and started conversation; unsurprisingly, a friendship sparked and became closely acquainted within a few weeks. All was going smoothly. Evelyn was learning the ropes of business under the direction of her father, Lord Lewis Moore, and Jacob began his first romance novel, titled: *That day in autumn*. Somewhere along the line, Jacob suspected Evelyn was catching feelings of affection for him too, and so his dreams of marriage began.

*

It was a blustery autumn day, and young Lockhart observed the woman he loved reading a book in St. James park. Her caramel brown hair and frilly burgundy dress swayed in the breeze. Her expression was whimsical and wondrous, it made the man question what she was daydreaming about.

Holding a dark crimson rose in his hands, the man adjusted his collars and began to walk in her direction. The first few steps he took were bouncy and full of glee, but slowly they slackened and hesitated, until the man was standing completely still. Another young man, who Jacob recognised as being Earl Charles Ethel, sat beside Evelyn and handed her a white rose. At first Jacob didn't understand... he was aware that Charles was also studying business, (only because he inherited the Ethel's tea company) but he didn't realise the two were acquainted. To the man's astonishment, Charles then took the girl's hand and planted a kiss on the back of it. The gesture boiled his blood, but he wasn't going to jump to conclusions without investigating further.

The next day, when the two were in the university library, Jacob questioned Evelyn about what he had witnessed. Giving a mixed look of disbelief and guilt, Evelyn went on to explain that she was to be engaged with Charles within a couple of months. Jacob felt his heart sink at those words, but resisted the urge to let the sorrow show on his face. Instead he smiled, and asked her what circumstances lead up to it all. Evelyn told him that her family were rather close with the

Ethel's, and back when she was a little girl, she and Charles were introduced. Since both families were of noble blood and took pride in their own companies, Evelyn and Charles' parents decided it was ideal for them to be wed. Jacob gave a frown, and said to the girl:

" Without you Evelyn, I will not have the inspiration to continue living."
Touched by Jacob's words, the girl thought long and hard for a way that meant they could still see each other, but in the end it was Jacob who came up with a solution.

The man worked, trained, and studied every day, until he was qualified enough to become the Ethel's head servant. Jacob's family were disappointed to see their son halt his original career plans to become a servant, but they were pleased he released a novel, even if it was his first and last debut. Seeing Charles every day of his life was unbearable for the butler, but his rage was always overthrown when he saw the happiness in Evelyn's bonnie brown eyes. For a couple of years, the man's life was tolerable, he actually got quite good at being a butler, and enjoyed some of the tasks he performed. It was only when Evelyn fell pregnant that his thoughts spiralled into hostility. If the child were a boy, he would one day become head of the household and would be able to rule over Jacob till the end of his days. If the child were a girl, she would only become head if she were the sole child, otherwise she would eventually get married and move on. Boy or girl, that child would be a symbol of Evelyn and Charles' love, and a constant reminder of how Jacob failed to win Moore's hand.

The days leading up to the child's birth was one of the butler's lowest points. He became increasingly bitter towards the nobility, and their dismissive attitudes towards others. Sometimes Jacob thought about terrible things. Things like exposing of Charles' corpse, things like having Evelyn plunge into the hands of despair so she would fall to his feet. On one occasion, he touched upon the thought of getting rid of the unborn child... but he never did. When the time came, and the new member of the Ethel family was born, tears arose in the butler's eyes. He observed the baby girl's sleeping features, and it melted his heart. The baby may have possessed her father's looks, but something about her resembled Evelyn so flawlessly.

As the baby grew, she became curious and lively, sharing the exact interests and traits as her loving mother. The girl had a passion for reading and writing, she immersed herself in nature, she was fascinated with music, but most of all, she was kind to everyone who was privileged enough to meet her. Though Jacob always thought Charles to be a curse, Paula became his blessing. Within a little space of time, she became incredibly dear to the butler. Even over her parents, Paula would choose to have a tea party with Jacob, write poems, or even practise the piano with him. The man's heart thawed, but only for Paula and Evelyn. As long as they never left his side, the man promised to play nice.

"Jacob, can we play Erik Satie today?"

The innocent little girl looked up from the piano seat (which was much too big for her), and smiled at her butler. Jacob grinned and sat the girl on his lap, he was no stranger to the piano and was more than happy to play for Paula. About midway through the melody, Jacob caught sight of Charles and Evelyn swooning over each other in the upstairs hall. Seemingly more irritated, Jacob instructed Paula to continue practising while he investigated the commotion. When Jacob wandered upstairs, the couple stopped twirling around and gave him a coy smile.

"Why, whatever is the cuffuffle, my lady?"

Turning her head to Charles, she waited to see a nod, then walked up to Jacob.

"I'm expecting again, and with God's grace, I believe it will be a boy."

Suddenly Jacob felt disgusted. This new child would spoil everything! In time he would end up taking over the manor, estate, and the business, meaning Paula will be off to be wed and out of his life forever! Not only that, but Charles and Evelyn's love was taking up so much space, that soon Jacob would become nothing more than a memory. Little by little, the butler's bitterness returned. Every time he saw *his* rightful lover kiss and embrace that lowly Ethel, his heart began to turn to stone, until one day his love for Evelyn perished. Nothing was holding him back now, nothing except Paula.

"Jacob, the Florist's ball is to be conducted later, can you please inform Ophelia to collect Paula from school today." The butler bowed, "Of course, mistress. Leave it to me..."

As soon as she left the kitchen, the crafty cogs in Jacob's head began to turn. The meeting of the *Floriographists* was held three times a year. All nobility who's family crest resembled flora gathered in attendance. Each floral crest resembled a particular trait, a violet of watchfulness for the Youngs, lupins of luck for the Stitchs, roses of love for the Ethels and whatnot. In the butler's eyes, it was just a ridiculous excuse for wealthy blood to come together for a gossip, but it did give him an opportunity. The Ethel parents would be alone, and away from Paula. With Paula out of harm's way, Jacob could put his plan into effect.

*

That morning started off like any other; Jacob got breakfast ready, swept the manor, went out for his daily errands, and got Paula ready for school. The man had assured the girl a tea-party with freshly made ginger biscuits after school. Oh, how he hated to break promises.

"See you shortly, my young lady."

Paula giggled, and hugged the butler's leg. The man patted the girl's head and waved her goodbye from the front door. As he turned around, the Ethel couple were dolling themselves up in velvet coats, and fancy gloves. Perhaps they were taking this meeting seriously. Well, that didn't matter.

Soon they wouldn't need to worry about business trips, meetings, or anything of that sort.

"OW!"

"Oh! My humble apologies, Clifford!"
The Ethel's popped their heads around the side of the carriage, and gasped when they saw the family driver, Clifford, clutching his hand in discomfort. Jacob had 'accidentally' shut the carriage door on his wrist, leaving his right hand utterly useless.

"Ah'm terribly sorry me lady, but Ah won't be able to drive the carriage like this."

"This won't do at all! You're the only person who knows the quickest directions we need to take."

A smile tugging the corner of his lips, Jacob bowed and stepped between Clifford and Evelyn. He proposed a splendid idea: He could take hold of the reins and direct the horses, while Clifford instructed the directions he'd need to take. After some second glances, everyone decided that was the best option, and just like that, the family was off on the road at last.

The coach ride was dull, and Jacob was beginning to feel paralysed. Sitting on the carriage's outer seat was utterly unbearable, he couldn't imagine doing this every time the master or mistress needed to venture out. No one said much, except for Clifford who occasionally shouted 'left', 'right', or 'drive on'. They passed meadows, roadside, and a few odd houses, until they reached the south-side of town. Ah yes, Stone-Arch bridge, famous, only because of the number of nobles that have graced its cobblestones. This was the place Jacob was waiting to reach-

With a violent movement, Jacob tugged onto the reins. The force was so brutal that one of the horses stood on its hind legs in trepidation and the other clumsily reversed itself against the bridge's low wall. The butler leaped from the driver's seat before the off-balanced carriage slid off the bridge's edge. One horse slid into the river, crushing Clifford as it fell, the other galloped into the nearby grove. Jacob looked down to see the coach rapidly filling up with water, Evelyn and Charles were bashing on the window, staring at him with mortified eyes.

"Tsk, tsk, tsk, what a nasty fall," he smiled to himself, amusement glinting in his eyes. "I better give them a hand!"

With some effort the butler pried the loose stones, making half the bridge collapse.

It was an easier task than he thought since the foundation was already eroding away. The stones crushed the carriage upon impact, making a clutter of debris float downstream.

"Alas, 'tis the curtain's call upon our villains, and the leading man cannot take to centre stage. Now, to find the understudy to take his place."

Jacob travelled into the grove, where the trees were dense and thick with moss. Wandering far enough to be concealed by the shrubbery, but close enough to see the pathway, the man pulled out a bloodied corpse from inside a hollow trunk. He was careful not to get blood on his best uniform, as he dragged the body by its hair. The corpse was fresh, and not yet stiff. It somehow resembled the butler. Jacob took the pin from his tailcoat and fixed it onto the corpse's breast pocket, then hauled the body into the river below and watched it float on the water's surface. After launching another few boulders into the water, a snarl spread across his face when he heard the corpse's skull crack. With one final glance at the carnage he created, the man took off into the woods. As the butler sprinted through the trees, he thought back to the 'errands' he performed earlier that day...

*

He told the Ethel's he was going to get his clothes mended by the tailor, little did they know that he actually went out to prepare. Jacob walked not to town, but to the very woods he was running through now. He hid amongst the bushes, and preyed upon unknowing travellers who were unfortunate enough to cross his path. A little girl and boy skipped past the butler's hiding spot, holding hands while whistling a pretty tune. A skinny woman with a basket of apples also strode past. Patience was a virtue, and soon the perfect person came strolling along. A well-built man with brunet hair and blue eyes crouched by the grove's edge and began to pick some bluebells. '*Well, his eyes wouldn't be much of an issue*', Jacob thought to himself as he took off his gloves.

The butler tackled the man, covering his mouth and trapping his neck between his arm. Once the man became winded, Jacob held the sides of his head and cracked the poor fellow's neck. The butler then took a hefty, jagged stone and smashed it against the man's face repetitively. His features needed to be near unrecognisable for the rest of the butler's scheme to work. After dressing the corpse in one of his own uniforms, he hid the body in a hollow tree. Jacob cleaned himself up and went back to the Ethel manor, readily awaiting his mistress.

*

Snapping from his recollections, the butler stopped at an abandoned cottage in the woods. It had been there ever since he was a young boy, but even he never met the previous owner. The home had been neglected and forgotten for a long while, which made it the perfect place for him to claim as his own.

For the next ten years, Jacob spent his days planning, preparing, and conjuring the next steps for his vision. The man had infiltrated other abandoned areas around London: the rundown clock tower in the outer fields, the graveyard chapel where no one dared enter, and the desolate factory which sat amongst the filthy alleys. Over the years he collected newspapers, and photographs of nobles and hung them on the walls of his home. The man was particularly pleased when he read the newspaper about the Ethel family's demise. He never wanted to lose that happy feeling, and so read it over and over again, never getting tired of that crumpled old bit of paper. It stated that Evelyn Ethel, Charles Ethel, Clifford Turner, and Jacob Lockhart were all dead. Jacob let out an insane chuckle as he began to scribble on the walls with red dye.

"Ha! I've done it, they all think I'm dead!

He took a paintbrush from the desk and drew a large circle around Paula's photograph.

"Oh, my dear sweet Eve-" he paused and smiled...

"My dear sweet Paula, as your butler I apologise for bringing so much heartache upon you, but you'll see...this is for your benefit."

The man then painted straight lines connecting Paula's photograph to several others.

"Let's see now, your parents were your biggest downfall but they are gone. Who's next? Ah yes, Eric Randal... he was friends with you, right?

Having finished his conversation with Paula's portrait, the old butler went out into the night in pursuit of Earl Eric Randal.

As Jacob reached the Randal estate he chuckled. Eric was a lonely man and therefore had no servants! How fortunate for him.

Jacob snuck past the manor's kitchen window; he caught sight of a dark-haired, doll-faced servant. He was preparing tea and baking something that looked quite appetising.

"Aww, one mere servant then. It warms my heart to see a butler care for his master with no ill will. It will really sting when the lad realises his failure to uphold his commitment."

With a snicker, the man stealthily ventured behind the house. The old brickwork of Eric's manor was atrocious, but it was a good blunder for Jacob. With ease, he climbed up the misplaced bricks and up to a curtained window. The butler realised the window wasn't locked, in fact, the hinges were broken from the inside. Having a large enough gap for him to peer through, Jacob found himself faced with the back of someone's head. From the picture frame placed on the man's desk, Jacob wagered it must be Eric. A twisted grin warped his lips; Jacob lunged out from behind the curtain and put a hand over Eric's mouth. He proceeded to stab the blonde in the back and neck.

"What a fragile lad you are, already loosing so much blood..."

With a few more violent jabs, the Earl's head fell on the desk with a thud. The killer escaped back to the woods and awaited the press printing the news.

This went on for years; the butler would kill any noble who had a connection with Paula, then be utterly delighted when their deaths were printed in the papers. Strangely enough other murders were reported on... but Jacob wasn't the one causing all the havoc. Seems like London was crawling with monsters of his kind.

Earl Randal needed to die because he fancied Paula when he was a young lad, Jacob was aware of this many years ago but finally decided to act upon it. Baron Keith also needed to be disposed of. Jacob never liked the way the old pervert looked at his innocent Paula, and so the deed was carried out. There were many others murdered, but when the butler heard about Miss Young's ball, he knew he needed to attend.

The ball itself was rather drab for his liking; the food was bland and the company was far too low for his standards. Jacob was glad it was a masquerade... he could weave amongst the crowds without drawing attention to himself. He was scouting out potential nobles he could erase, but instead his eyes found the beautiful Paula Ethel. For some moments it was as if time stood still, from such a sweet little girl to a gorgeous young lady. For the first time in a long while the man was speechless. Suddenly, the grin on his face faded. Who was that sitting with her? Another butler? If that wasn't enough to rattle his bones, then Alister Knox kissing the back of her hand was. Just when the killer reached for his gun, Audrey grasped Alister's hand and kissed his cheek fondly. Jacob let his hand fall as he looked at the couples dancing under the golden chandelier.

"Time for some chaos..." he whispered to himself.

After the whole 'Masquerade Massacre' incident, Jacob murdered another: Viscount Landers. He only killed him because the old codger disrespected Paula's piano solo at one of the Ethel's renowned garden parties. For cutting her dreams in two, the old man paid the ultimate fee. The butler also managed to nab Duke Alister Knox. Now he was a tricky one... for the longest time Jacob tormented the duke at the deserted clock tower; he still wasn't sure what to do with him.

"So, *Twisted Jester* is what society calls me then, eh?"
Alister mumbled and cried while being gagged with an old piece of cloth.

"What's that? You don't want me to kill you?
The duke furiously shook his head.

"Hmm... alright then. I think I know what do with you now."

Later that evening, Jacob dragged the cyanide dosed duke to the Ethel's garden. The butler threw him to the ground and beat him till bruises erupted on his face. After clawing at him with leaves of poison ivy, the man stepped back and admired his handy work.

"Don't worry, my poor lad. I won't murder you, actually you will be perfect bait to strike fear into others of your kind. Besides you're not in love with Paula, right? Your heart belongs to Audrey, yes?"
Over Alister's groans and howls, Jacob heard another man's voice shout 'Mistress'.

Taking out his golden bordered pocket watch, Jacob brushed his thumb against the etched letters 'J, L, L' and studied the time.

"My, my, would you look at the time. I do believe I should take my leave. But do give Audrey my best."

With a bow, the old butler left the near-lifeless man amongst the blades of grass for Paula to find. He was getting quite agitated by the fact that the other nobles and servants continuously hovered around *his* mistress; but if they weren't going to step aside, then Jacob would just have to take her.

*

A few days later, Jacob returned to the Ethel estate. After breaking into the manor and stealing Clement's clothing, he went to Cliffe's house and told him to take the carriage to the north-side tea house. It was easy to access the manor, as the butler had cleverly held onto the house key he received from Evelyn all those years ago. He knew Ophelia wouldn't think to change the locks. It was even easier to trick such pathetic servants. Cliffe was just as dense as his dear father Clifford was. With the carriage on its way to the Ethel's tea house, Jacob returned the borrowed items of clothing to the rear pantry and ventured into the grove closest to the manor. He'd been watching Paula from afar, and wagered she would come outside prior to her little tantrum. Ambushing her was both difficult and exhilarating. For a bit of a scare, Jacob skimmed his dagger down her back, and just as he predicted, the girl fainted out of fear. Having Paula fall into his arms brought a smile to his face. At last butler and mistress were reunited, but Jacob wasn't stopping there.

The man brought Paula to his hideout. He had no intention of revealing his true self, or to kill anyone else. He simply wanted the girl to himself.

"Young mistress, look how much you've grown...you are your mother's spitting image."

Much like when Jacob was talking to Paula's portrait, he now twirled around her unconscious body and made small talk.

"You must have been utterly heartbroken without me, right? Oh, the fun we used to have."

Still staring at her sleeping features, the butler brushed away her curly fringe to reveal a fresh graze. He scowled as he realised how careless he was carrying her body here. His eyes broadened when a drop of blood ran down the side of her head, and another memory flooded his mind...

"Jacob, I cut my finger."
The butler turned around to see a teary-eyed Paula holding out a bloodied hand. Under her other arm was a dismantled music box; the handle was loose and the cylindrical mechanism that spun the tune had snapped off.
"Now, how did you manage to accomplish such a thing?"
The crying child didn't give an answer and instead stepped closer to the kneeling butler. Jacob took her hand to get a better look at the cut. It wasn't a messy wound, just a straight incision which was a little deeper than he originally thought. The man just parted his lips to say something when a perfect droplet of blood ran down Paula's finger to her palm. The bright red liquid contrasted so well with the girl's skin; it was strangely satisfying, like watching a glass full of red wine spill all over a cream tablecloth. The butler tightened his grip around the girl's wrist and for a moment madness shone in his eyes...
"Jacob?"

At once the butler regained his composure and ignored the thought of young Paula looking at him with such guiltless eyes. He observed the real Paula, tied up helplessly in front of him. It was apparent, even now her rich blood contrasted with her beauteous skin.

"Some things don't change...."

Jacob muttered to himself. The man noticed that Paula's eyelids began to discreetly move. Without hesitation, he placed his Jester's mask back on his face and stood in close proximity to the girl's person. Unsurprisingly, Paula was terrified when she awoke, staring straight in the face of the devil himself. The man slid two fingers under her chin, trying to get a closer look at her stunning beauty. To his disgrace, Paula hissed and aggressively turned away.

Jacob didn't appreciate that. If Paula was going to behave in such an impolite manner, then he had no choice but to punish her. He proceeded into the other room where all his tools were stocked. Taking out a dagger he went back to the girl's thigh and began to slice her. '*Do good and receive rewards, do bad and receive punishment*' that was Jacob's firm belief from the very beginning. It may have been a harsh punishment for the girl, but Jacob certainly felt rewarded. My... what a gorgeous form she possessed. The girl squirmed and struggled each time the blade's cold tip would slice into her supple skin. Immersed in his own fantasies, Jacob hadn't noticed someone unlocking the door behind him.

When a fine, young gentleman burst into the room, an ugly scowl appeared on Jacob's lips. Of course, no one could tell he was glaring because of the wide smile plastered onto his mask.

It was the Ethel's new butler, again?

"Ugh, what a pain in the arse this servant is becoming."

This man, this heroic butler was there during the ball, he was there to save Alister from his sticky fate, and to top it all off, he was constantly coddling Paula. For a split-second Jacob squinted through his mask and realised he had met this man before. Wasn't this man Randal's butler? The killer wanted to burst out into laughter, but with Thomas charging at him with so much determination, he decided to make a swift escape. Slipping a bit when he jumped out the window, Jacob looked back to the factory and saw Thomas' silhouette looking in his direction. Jacob ran to his next hideout, the desolated chapel, and hoped he could come up with another plan to abduct Paula.

After another few days Jacob decided on his next move. It was his last resort, something the butler wanted to avoid, but desperate times called for desperate measures. Paula didn't want him any more, she was disgusted by him, all she wanted was 'Thomas'. The thought made Jacob's fists clench, but if it was true, then Paula needed to die. If Jacob killed Paula with his own hands then she would become his for eternity. Even in death... the old butler imagined how lovely the girl would be.

Later that night Jacob emerged from the cemetery grounds, the lunacy in his eyes more potent than ever before. He returned to the Ethel's for a third time, but he was no longer interested in mediocre games. Wasting no time breaking-in from Paula's window, he was ready to strike her through the back all the way to her heart. The adrenaline coursing through him drained when he caught sight of Thomas once again, this time coming at him with nothing but sheer ferocity. Even Jacob admitted a slither of fear crawled into his mind when Thomas made chase.

Jacob kept running. The numbing cold, the wind clawing his face, the snow piled at his knees, nothing stopped him from running away from Thomas. He looked around and his eyes grew wide at his surroundings, he was standing on the Stone-Arch bridge; the very place where this insanity started. When Thomas cornered him, Jacob tried to strike him down but... he missed. He missed! The great Jacob Lester Lockhart? A pain swelling in the man's chest, he didn't muster any more of his will to stab Thomas. A little voice inside him, a voice he formerly believed to be extinct, told him he was bested. With nothing more to give, Jacob thought at least one person should know his secret. [11]Gently peeling away his mask, he waited to see Thomas' features contort and twist, and only then did he let himself fall backwards.

The man thought the fall would be rapid and over in an instant, but for some reason or another, he descended kindly. As a boy, he tended to daydream and get lost in

---

[11] It is recommended to play the instrumental version of Tom Piper's Son for this scene.

old memories, but why now of all times was he remembering them? A vision of his parents came to mind, his uncle, another memory of the struggles he faced when he was writing his novel, followed by an illusion of Evelyn with flushed cheeks. Just as tears began brimming the surface of his emerald eyes, a memory of little, sweet Paula came to mind...

"Jacob... even if I run over the hills and far away, promise me you'll still be here when I come back, promise me... okay?"

The young girl smiled as she skipped down the pavement with a bundle of books under her arm. She waved in the distance, but didn't once look away from her butler. All of a sudden, Jacob remembered how much he hated to break promises...

Chapter 14

Lock and key

"Thomas! Thomas what did you see?" said Paula.

The butler sat upright, staring at the empty velvet seat in front of him. His cheeks and nose were bright pink, and his skin was as cold as ice.

"Thomas, say something!"

He could very well hear his mistress shouting beside him, but no matter how much he tried, no words escaped his mouth. Cliffe pulled up alongside the Ethel manor and assisted Paula with getting the traumatised man out of the carriage.

"Mr Fulton?" Cliffe patted the man's arm.

"For heaven's sake Thomas!" Paula yelled.

The butler crooked his head and stared down at Paula. He gulped, his lips quivering as he spoke.

"Mistress... the Jester- he..."

"What? What has he done to you?" The butler swallowed some air, his mouth as dry as a desert.

"Mistress... I k-know who the Jester was," the butler swallowed, "I- It was Jacob."

There was a sudden pause. Paula studied her butler's blanched face.

"What? You can't really mean 'that' Jacob?"

Thomas tossed his head to the side; he couldn't bare facing the young woman knowing the truth. His silence spoke volumes, and even though the mere thought of Jacob Lockhart being the Twisted Jester made the girl's skin crawl, she trusted Thomas. Paula didn't believe her butler would tell a jest, let alone, tell such a horrid lie.

"H- how did you know it was him?" Paula immediately regretted asking that question.

Thomas' hand shook slightly.

"It was that photograph. The one in that book."

The picture of Jacob in his butler's uniform. An air of grace around him, a sweet smile on his face. Who knew that Jacob would become-

Paula stopped thinking. She looked at her butler... it was the first time she had seen him this fearful. The girl didn't enquire any further, she knew he would need to re-tell the events to the police and, for both their sakes, she would rather only hear the story once.

Surprisingly, it was Clement who took the liberty of calling the police, despite the fact that his conversation was mostly panicked gibberish. The officers arrived with haste when they heard the name *Twisted Jester*. Thomas, Paula, and Cliffe entered the manor to the sound of familiar voices. Christa ushered the three of them to the parlour where Clement was chatting with the same pair of officers from before. The officers stood when Paula entered, and, by observing the disturbed look on her face, didn't waste time with formalities.

The light-haired policeman looked in the servant's direction; trying to get them to leave. Paula stepped in and stood between Christa and Clement.

"This concerns all of us," Paula boldly stated.

Studying the stern expression on the lady's face, both officers sat back down and gestured for the servants to do the same. Everyone took a seat and one-by-one began to tell all they knew regarding the Jester and his ploy. Both men asked the occasional question, all while scribbling away on bits of paper. After more than an hour of being interviewed, the two policemen had a pile of pages, but despite all that was written, there was nothing concerned with the Jester's motives. They knew Jacob attacked nobles specifically, and that he had a deeper connection with the Ethel's but, with little evidence as to why he committed it all, they theorised he must have done it out of jealousy or spite.

Everyone in the room took a moment to let the information sink in. Previously, no one could rest without knowing the truth behind London's gruesome murders, but now each one of them discovered something; the only thing worse than knowing too little was knowing too much. Never, not even with all the wisdom in the world, would the Ethel's have guessed the deranged, heartless, inhumane Jester could be the intelligent, loving, sympathetic Jacob.

"Thank you all for your co-operation. A short while before you arrived Miss Paula, we sent an inspector to Stone-Arch bridge, you will be receiving a letter regarding what he found in a couple of days."

"Thank you again, Sirs."

Both policemen lifted themselves from their chairs.

"Of course, if you find any other information concerning this case, do not hesitate to contact us."

Paula nodded; her servants did the same. After folding the notes in a case the policemen left to hear word from the investigators. Immediately after the front door shut, the servants started to bombard Paula and Thomas with a whirlwind of questions.

"My lady, why did you run off on your own?" Christa spoke while folding her arms.

"Thomas mate! How'd you know the Jester was gonna strike again?" Clement questioned, dumbfounded.

"Me lady, Am sorry Ah couldn't do more to help ya," Cliffe frowned.

Paula and Thomas were already so exhausted, and all the shouting wasn't helping their condition at all. Despite all the hardship the butler went through, he mustered his remaining might to settle the other servants down.

"Now, now, there's no need to become so excitable. The mistress has had a long day and she's in no shape to answer your questions."

The three servants lumbered about with embarrassment. Then, after an instant of reflecting, they bowed and apologised. Thomas exhaled and clapped his hands together.

"Right, we should all retire for the night and pick up discussion tomorrow."

"Right you are, Thomas," the three of them said simultaneously.

The chef and the gardener bowed and made their way to their quarters. Cliffe also bowed and placed his hat atop his head. The butler saw the driver to the door and after he was out of sight, Thomas focused his attention on Paula.

"Off you go, my lady. You need to sleep now."

The girl gave a nod then gradually began to walk up the stairs. She looked utterly lost, like a frightened rabbit who'd been separated from its mother. Of course, Thomas wasn't expecting Paula to be jovial and cheery, how could she be? Yes, the case might be solved, but the truth cut a wound deeper than any of the physical scars on her body.

Standing in the corridor, looking up to the shadowy stairwell, the butler wondered if his mistress would ever be the same again.

*

Two months had passed since The Twisted Jester's case had been closed. Paula received a follow up letter regarding what the police found at stone-arch bridge; it specified that an eight-inch dagger was found buried in the snow as well as a torn piece of Thomas' tailcoat. Paula's heart began to race when she discovered Thomas was struck; it was just dumb luck that the dagger impaled his clothes and not his flesh. The letter also stated that no footprints, nor that the body was found. The investigators reckoned the corpse must have floated downstream, or, on a grislier note, could have broken-up into myriads of pieces since it was frozen solid. The thought terrified the young woman. She could never receive closure since Jacob's body may never be recovered, but Thomas reassured her time and time again that being frozen to the blood and bones left no chance of ever waking up.

It was up to the law and the nobles to clean up the Jester's mess. With the power and money both these parties possessed, they could easily revert society's attention away from the recent killings and towards something light-hearted. The officers completed and closed all murder cases linked to the Jester; this included the Ethel family's case and Earl Eric Randal's. Nobles such as Audrey, Archie, and of course, Paula, arranged a spring festival to lift the spirits of the community and send a message of new beginnings. It was a huge success, for the first time in a long time the under-classes and upper-classes alike looked truly content.

Aside from all the merry making, there was another reason to be joyful: Alister's condition was rejuvenating. No longer was his skin swollen and bruised and, with some additional support from Doctor Farthing, he was gradually speaking again. No one was more thankful than Audrey, at last she could hear her lover's voice again. The experience of almost losing the man she loved made Audrey realise life was fleeting, and for this reason the girl made a grand decision: she was going to marry the duke.

Sunday morning came around quickly. The servants gathered around the garden table and went about their daily business, Christa and Clement were facing it off in a game of chess, Thomas was reading complicated looking sheet music, and Paula was checking the morning papers. The spring air was bountiful; the fragrance of wildflowers, lush grass, and sweet fruits wafted along with the warm breeze. Paula inhaled deeply and let the fresh air fill her lungs. Feeling revived, the girl continued to skim through the pile of papers, her face lit up when she stumbled upon an invitation.

"Well I never..." said Paula.

Noticing the smile creeping onto her face, the servants halted their activities and sat up with anticipation.

"What is it, mistress?" Clement asked. Paula flipped the invite and displayed it to the three curious servants.

"An invitation to Lady Audrey and Duke Alister's wedding," Paula smiled.

"A wedding? Sounds like right fun!" Clement beamed.

"Indeed, it does sound nice. You and Thomas would be attending then?" Christa enquired.

Paula looked over to her butler.

"You'll come with me, right?"

The butler chuckled lightly.

"Of course, I wouldn't miss it for the world, my lady."

The butler's sweet response put the girl's mind at ease. Truth be told, Paula would have felt nervous going to Audrey's manor on her own, she was still paranoid from all the previous tragedies. Reading the date on the envelope, Paula was pleasantly surprised to see that the wedding was to be held the following Sunday morning at St Andrew's church. The young woman smiled to herself; she had a feeling this wedding would be one to remember.

*

"How do I look?"
Paula whispered to Thomas, who was placing a present on the gift table.

"You look beautiful, my lady. You always look beautiful."

Paula's rosy cheeks went unnoticed by the flocks of guests bustling around the banquet table and far-off visitors rushing to get front row seats, but to Thomas, it was the only thing he could concentrate on. The church was modestly decorated in white and navy-blue themed décor, (navy being both Audrey and Alister's favourite colour). For this reason, Paula was wearing a cerulean frilled dress with white flowers at the base, and Thomas was wearing a cobalt-shaded tie with a white rose poking out of his breast pocket.

"Ladies and gentlemen, if you would please take your seats, the service will commence shortly," said the churchman.

Paula and her butler made their way to the second row and sat on the seats closest to the aisle. Some people were still silently murmuring amongst themselves, while others were scoffing treats they had swiped from the banquet table. Paula looked to the altar where Alister was adjusting his bow tie, they both caught sight of each other, and the duke gave a kind nod. There was something in his twinkling eyes, appreciation? Gratitude? It was probably a combination of emotions- this was his wedding after all! The church doors opened, and curious heads turned around all at once.

It wasn't Audrey, it was a handful of nobles which Paula recognised. Better late than never, she supposed. The embarrassed few filled the gaps in the benches and scrambled to any empty seat they could find, amongst them was Earl Archie. The blonde man squeezed passed Thomas and took a seat next to Paula.

"Sorry about the intrusion, Miss Paula."

"Not at all, Mr Stitch. Glad you could join us."

The man brushed some lint off his sapphire jacket and smiled at the girl.

"You would not believe the fuss outside, barely enough space for a carriage."

Archie sighed, then his eyes landed to the altar. Alister mouthed something to him and the earl chuckled under his breath. Paula guessed Alister was relieved to find his trusted friend had made it to his ceremony. But who really knew? Men laugh about the strangest of things sometimes.

The door made a creek and again anticipating heads turned around. A little girl in a white dress came skipping down the aisle, scattering pink petals on the red carpet below. Thomas recognised her as the young girl he saw at Bridgedale. Beside her was a little black-haired boy wearing a smart blue jacket, he was carrying a basket of white rose petals, but he was tossing them more on the guests than the carpet. After the children finished layering the floor with mellow, sweet-smelling flowers, the orchestra began to play.

Audrey walked in, gracefully, elegantly, her ginger hair was tied in a curly up-do and her dress was so white it was blinding. As she got closer to the altar, Alister took in a breath and looked like he was about to fall to tears. Audrey stood opposite her fiancé and lifted

the translucent veil over her head. The priest
began the service and the whole room
hushed. The vows were said and the rings
were exchanged. When it came to the kiss,
Alister took his bride's hand and kissed the
back of it, a gracious move indeed. The
church bells began to ring and an eruption of
cheers and hats went flying. All the while,
Paula felt a pair of eyes watching her. She
subtly turned her head to Thomas who was
giving her a longing look.

"What is it, Thomas?"

The butler didn't say anything, he just
plucked the white rose from his pocket and
tucked it behind Paula's flushed ear. The
girl's pink checks were hidden by all the
petals and ribbons flying through the air. She
was right, this was certainly going to be a
wedding to remember...

*

Back at the Ethel manor, the mistress and
butler were greeted with an immaculate front
room. Wandering around to the hall and into
the dining room, Paula and Thomas were
astounded with how tidy everything was.

"Christa! Clement! Where are you
both?" Thomas said.

The two energetic servants emerged from the kitchen. The gardener had soot on her cheek and forehead, and the chef had pine leaves sticking out of his hair.

"Welcome back, mistress!" They both said.

It seemed like the two were planning this from the start. They were as thoughtful as ever.

"Good evening you two. It looks as though you have switched jobs," said Paula

Christa put her hand over her face and observed the soot marks on the tips of her fingers. Clement plucked a leaf from his hair and was a bit startled when in snapped in half. They all glanced at each other then burst out laughing.

"We were having a competition you see, trying to figure out who's better at doing chores," Christa explained.

"Well, I'd say both of you are matched. The manor looks beautiful, well done you two," Thomas smiled, chuffed.

The servants looked stunned for a moment. Receiving praise from Thomas was like been given a chest full of jewels. There was nothing in the world they enjoyed more than the feeling of a job-well-done.

"Thank you, Thomas!" They both shouted.

The evening went by as pleasantly as they did when Paula was a little girl. The three servants and their mistress had dinner early for a change and then decided to immerse themselves in something leisurely. The chef and the gardener went outside to the orchard, where they were hoping the plums had grown and ripened. Paula insisted that they may not be ripe enough yet, but that didn't stop the two from trying. Meanwhile, Thomas deciphered the sheet music and was thrilled he could finally relay the notes to Paula. Feeling the piano under her fingers again, the girl felt oddly nostalgic. It hadn't been that long since she last played, but the sensation was more comforting somehow.

"Alright mistress, today we are going to play *Nocturne in E Flat Major* by Chopin."

Thomas placed the sheet of music on the piano stand. Paula scanned the melody, then took a deep breath. The tune was slow and soothing, as serene as the melodies she played in the past. As the girl continued to play, Thomas began to wonder...

The Jester, no, Jacob, had a limitless revulsion for nobles; Thomas may not have known why that loathing came to be, but he did know it went against all the butler's oaths. From what Thomas found out, it was never Lockhart's intention to become a butler; it was just something he decided on a whim. Through Jacob's eyes, nobles were something to capture and dispose of, that is where Thomas differed. The man always dreamed of becoming a fully-fledged servant. Through Thomas' eyes his role was to care for his master, cultivate them into becoming the best they could possibly be and help them discover their dreams. That was a butler's duty, and the man would carry his obligation till the very end.

"How was that, Thomas?"
The butler reverted from his daydream and bowed.

"It was a beautiful tune mistress, very emotional."

The girl tilted her head and smiled. Deep down, Paula knew she would have never recovered from all the trauma if her butler wasn't by her side. She stood up from the piano seat and walked over to the sculptured man. She gave a fond look and inched closer to him. Just as Paula was about to say something, a noise came from the front door. Both of them looked a bit alarmed.

"I'll see who it is, mistress."

Thomas ventured to the front door and opened it carefully. Out of nowhere a little ball of caramel fluff lunged at him, making him fall to the floor. It smelled of rain, had muddy paws, and dropped something from between its teeth.

"Ah, my lady! We seem to have a visitor."

Paula entered the hallway and fell into giggles, "Oh, what a gorgeous turnspit hound!"

The turnspit puppy[12] immediately ran up to Paula, jumping up to rest its paws on the hem of her dress.

"Oh my, what a mess you are..." Paula stroked behind the pup's ears.

"What's a sweet little thing like you doing so far out here?"

The hound whined and barked once. Thomas took his chance to get up and examine what the puppy had dropped.

"It's a collar of some sort..."

---

[12] Turnspit dogs were commonly used to rotate roasts over a fire by running on a wheel to keep the meat cooking evenly. The breed eventually went extinct in 1901 as mechanised spits became more common.

Paula took the collar from Thomas and turned it over.

"Belonging to C.E? Is that perhaps the initials of the owner?"

"It could be my lady. This puppy must have ran away."

Paula hauled up the turnspit in her arms, saddened to think such a gorgeous breed could belong to someone else.

"Well... perhaps we should bathe and feed her before her owner comes looking."

Before Thomas could answer, Paula already began to take the dog away to the back porch. She got an old wooden washtub ready with warm water and placed the hound inside. It seemed like the furry creature enjoyed the warmth.

"My lady we found some..."

Christa and Clement returned from the orchard.

"...Plums..."

"Eh, mistress. I didn't know ya had a mut," Clement said.

Paula giggled, "It's not mine, she just sort of- ahh"-

The hound splashed and played, wagging its tail happily, making everyone smile.

"She just sort of showed up," continued Paula.

"I'll get some milk for her," Christa said.

"Oh! I have an old quilt she can have!" Clement dropped the plums and ran inside.

"My, my, this puppy's stirring quite the fuss," Thomas said while also getting a towel to dry the little thing off with.

A few moments later they all sat in the kitchen. The puppy had drank some fresh milk, had warmed up by the fire and now sat curled in Clement's old quilt.

"Now, mistress... Don't get too attached to the thing."
Paula nodded but stroked the puppy's ears again.

Suddenly, another noise came at the door. Three distinct knocks.

"Look, that could be the turnspit's owner," said Thomas.
Paula got up, "I'll come too. I want to know who was careless enough to let her runaway."

They went to the front entrance and saw a silhouette outside the door. Thomas went ahead and opened the door. Both of them were surprised to see a familiar, composed face.

"Hello, Paula dear."

Ophelia stood on the other side, slight rain falling around her, hands bound together in front of her burgundy dress, hair tied back, as neat as ever. Her purple signet ring glinted in the moonlight, as did her glowing sapphire eyes.

"I have some matters I need to discuss with you, dear."

"*Matters...?*"

Bonus story

Teacups and bonbons

"You've done quite well for yourself, Charles."

"Thank you Richard, but I couldn't have accomplished such a thing without the help of your confectioners."

Both men, Charles Ethel and Richard Randal, analysed the teashop, nodding on occasion, admiring their handy work.

As the name rightly implied, *Ethel's Tea House* belonged to Charles. It was handed-down to the man by his father, Finley. But as the frail gentleman was nearing retirement he had no choice but to entrust the business to someone who was more able. Losing his sense of taste was also fatal for Finley whose livelihood depended on his ability to critique different teas and sweets. Fortunately, Charles was quite gifted when it came to sampling products. He could match the delicate flavours of tea with just the right sweet treat with ease, but when it came to the actual creation of the food, he lagged significantly. This is where Richard stepped-in. Having his own branches in the art of confectionery and baking, he was more than qualified to help Charles' business thrive.

"I only need five percent," Richard said.

His serious façade broke and the two men began to chuckle. The reason for their amusement flew right over their children's heads, who were looking up at them with confused faces. Charles' daughter, Paula, was a dainty little thing who was a spitting image of him. On the other hand, Eric, Richard's son, didn't share much of his father's looks, yet he did possess the same eager spirit.

Eric watched as Paula's curious eyes scanned the rows of cakes and jars of boiled sweets. The boy tugged on his father's sleeve and pointed to the jar of strawberry bonbons.

"Do you think we should treat them?" He turned to Charles.

"By all means. They have been rather patient," Charles smiled warmly.
Richard tipped a scoop of bonbons into a decorative bag.

"Here you are, my boy."

He placed the goods in the palm of Eric's hand, then continued his discussion with Charles. Eric waddled-up to Paula and offered her a sweet.

"They're really tasty," he said quietly.

Paula popped the sweet in her mouth, her cheeks turning a happy shade of pink when the mild strawberry flavour hit the back of her tongue. Eric hesitantly lifted a hand to the girl's face and gently prodded the blush.

"You look like a strawberry bonbon... are the sweets magic?"

Just as Paula's whole face turned red, the shop bell rang and caught both children off guard.

"Good morning, my lords."

A woman in a feathery hat and a little boy wearing a miniature cravat entered the shop. The boy acknowledged the presence of the other two children in the room, but didn't say anything until his mother spoke.

"Lady Stitch, how lovely to see you," Richard gave a slight bow.

"I'm so pleased you arrived early," Charles said.

The lady put a hand on the little boy's shoulder.

"You can thank my dear Archie for that. He's been pleading me to buy him some of your teacakes all morning," she laughed.

Charles knelt down to face Archie.

"You have good taste, my boy."

The man ushered Archie's attention to the glass counter which was protecting the treasures he sought: shelves and shelves of round cakes, pound cakes, stodgy puddings, chocolate rolls, and of course, teacakes. Archie gulped in anticipation.

"Well sweetheart, which cake do you fancy?"

Prompted by his mother's enthusiasm, Archie picked out a chocolate roll.

"That all?"

The boy looked at his mother than acknowledged the other two children again. He noticed the bag of pink bonbons in the other boy's hand and the sweet expression the girl was wearing.

"Can I have a slice of strawberry sponge as well?"

"I don't see why not," his mother smiled.

Mrs Stitch and Charles made an exchange, a slice of strawberry sponge and a creamy chocolate roll for five pennies. Archie rested the cakes on a pretty cloth, then waited for his mother to strike up conversation. Just as he hypothesised, as soon as Charles put the pennies in the register the three adults started talking again. It must have been something terribly boring because Archie's ears prevented him from hearing any of it.

The boy treaded carefully with his cakes and approached Paula and Eric.

"My name is Archie. That must be your father or uncle, right?" Archie discreetly pointed to Charles.

Eric laughed, "The man with the brown jacket is my father. He made the cake you're holding."

Archie took a bite of the chocolate roll, eyeing the boy. Eric stuffed his sweets in his pocket and held out his hand.

"My name is Eric by the way. I'm going to be in charge of my father's business when I'm all grown up, then I'll make all sorts of cake."

"I see."

Archie took a handkerchief from his pocket and dabbed the sides of his mouth, before shaking Eric's hand.

"And you?" He stared at Paula. Paula was usually quite shy. But perhaps that shyness was more toward adults, not children and so, she answered quickly.

"My name's Paula, and my father owns all the Ethel tea houses in London."

"Ah, so you two aren't siblings," said Archie.

"No! Of course not." Eric huffed. Archie smiled, "My mistake."

He stepped closer to Paula and held out the strawberry sponge.

"Care for some, Miss Paula?"
The girl stuttered, "I c-can't... that would be impolite of me."

"Well, my mother says when two people get acquainted it's nice to share something."

Archie broke the cake in two and handed the slice with more jam and sugar powder to Paula. She took a bite. It was delicious, not too sickly, not too dry, it was nice and balanced. Suddenly, she understood why her father sang Mr Randal's praises.

"It's delicious. Thank you, Archie."
Archie and Paula grinned at each other. Eric huffed again, making sure Archie noticed.

"Sorry, I thought you wouldn't want any. Your father makes these all the time, right?" Archie patted the other boy's shoulder.

Eric furrowed his brows and took the bonbons out of his pocket. He dipped a hand in the bag and realised all that delectable strawberry powder had been smeared all over his fingers. Curse this shop for being so stuffy, and these sweets for being so sticky, and curse Archie for appearing at the worst possible times, he thought.

He looked down at his hands again, frowning as he knew he would be scolded for covering himself in deep strawberry red stains...

Bonus Story

I found her at the port

I found her at the port. She was fascinated with the ships, or at least, the crates the ships were carrying.
      "Ophelia?"
She turned around, frightened, averting her gaze from the crates.
      "F-Finely...?"

                        *

It took me months to muster the courage to follow her. We saw each other a lot in the day but in the evenings, she would quite often, disappear.

Her father was a wine dealer, I started a tea company; naturally, we did business. But I found it queer... how his daughter would always be present, would be in the wine shop with him. Then, in my late twenties I travelled to China, and there she was, with her father again. I visited the country to buy some hand-crafted tea sets, they had come to trade liquor. It amazed me; how a woman could do so much, why her brother wasn't here in her place, what business she had talking with Chinese diplomats. But, I didn't ask questions. I was captivated by her soul. What a woman she was.

"You help your father regularly, do you?" I remember saying.

She laughed, "Oh yes, no one else was up for the job, but I can do anything."

"Well, I suppose going abroad a lot would be tedious."

I didn't know it at the time, but it wasn't the going abroad part of the job she was referring to, and she meant it when she said, she can do anything.

Only a few months had passed but I was completely taken with Ophelia. Her father liked the kind of lad I was growing into and he wanted us engaged. Ophelia was always pleasant with me, I dare say perhaps she fancied me too, but whenever the two of us seemed to be getting closer, she would always put up a wall.

"My apologies, Finely. I have to leave the ball early."

"Why ever for, my dear?" I stared at her, concerned.

She put one of her hands in mine, "I just- I must go."

Before giving me a chance to respond, she turned on her heels and fled. Staggering through the clusters of noble men and woman, she went out the front doors, and disappeared into the misty evening.

This had happened so many times before, but things were different now, we were engaged. It's that night I decided it was my right to find out what that woman was up to.

I excused myself from Viscount Lander's party. He was one of my regulars, and so thankfully, he took no offence to me taking my leave early. I reached the gates of Lander's estate before the rain started to fall.

"What a silly girl, taking off with a storm brewing overhead."
I was vexed. I had no idea where she could be. Her father wasn't in the country at this time. He was doing business in India and abruptly took Ophelia's brother with him. Could she be with her mother? No, she would have told me if that were the case.

"Where could you be..." I buried my face in my hands and caught a whiff of something...sea salt?

Now it all made sense to me. My lady loved the port, she would go there with her father, she would talk about how wonderful the ships were. Even at the beginning of our courtship we walked along the beach together.

I started to run, the clouds above becoming more and more ferocious. I was glad the ball was being held close to the shore, so it didn't take me too long to arrive. To my astonishment I was correct, there Ophelia was, standing on the quay. There was a man with her, but from the way they were standing, they must have been complete strangers.

"You can't pull a fast one on me girly, not enough shillings here," he said.

"My father dealt with you before, he gave you more than enough for you efforts." The man took a step closer and grinned, "Well, maybe if your father had acquainted me with you on our trade, I wouldn't have cared about being under-paid."

He suddenly took her wrist making me run toward her faster. Before I could react further, Ophelia clenched her fist and boxed his jaw. He recoiled and spat on the dock.

"Oh, you're goanna pay for that!" The man pushed her to the floor, but Ophelia only got up and swung at him again. Before I knew it they were fighting like ruffians.

"Ophelia!"

I reached her, grabbing the man by his arm and pushing him off the dock. He fell into the cold waters with a mighty splash. He crawled back onto dry land a few moments later.

"If you ever touch her again, I won't spare you. Now get out of my sight," I said. His head was bleeding a little. He had such hate in his eyes, but I could tell he had no fight left.

"Whatever you say, sir." The man dragged himself on a boat and it started to sail soon after.

"I do fine on my own," she said, dusting herself down.

I turned to Ophelia, holding her shoulders.

"Ophelia, look at you. You're bleeding, you're hurt... would you kindly tell me what's going on."

For the first time I saw tears in her eyes.

"Finely... I"-

Before she could speak a packet dropped from her pocket. She tried to swipe it before me but I picked it up and turned away.

"A packet of...?"

I read over the label: '*Opium, A woman's best friend'*, it read.

"Finely... It's just a medicine," she finally said.

"Medicine? Tell that to the people dying of the stuff!"

She stared at me and I couldn't help but feel sorry for her. What a state she was in, what mess she had tangled herself into. But no matter what, she was my Ophelia, my wife to be. I took a handkerchief and wiped away some blood on her cheek, I tucked back her hair and held her hands in mine.

"I don't care what you've done, but promise me you'll leave it behind you now." She couldn't look me in the eyes so I continued...

"Marry me. Marry me and you won't have to do this kind of business. You can run the tea company with me, it's doing well enough to see us and our future children through."

I got to see her cry and blush in the same night. She rested her head on my shoulder and sobbed.

"Okay, Finely. I will. I will marry you and forget about all this..."

We stayed in each other's grasp, listening to the waves brush against the shore. No matter what kind of dealings Ophelia was involved in, I was proven that night that she could hold her own. What a woman she was, indeed.

Sample

The book is over you say? Not quite... enjoy this little peak at the prequel:

The name Lockhart is so unfortunate, so dismal, almost always ending in something troublesome, but whether I liked it or not I was one. Jacob Lockhart, the boy with a stone heart, a barren heart, a locked heart.

I sat at the edge of *Stone-Arch bridge*, a bridge which connected the noble's private estates with the cramped Southside of London town. I looked to the left; fancy manors, gated gardens, and land the size of football pitches shot me ghastly gazes. I looked to the right; narrow streets, cluttered shop fronts, and rows of grey roofs called me back to their dingy clutches. I let my legs dangle a while longer, eyeing my reflection in the water far below. I wiped away a bit of dirt from my cheek, but in doing so marked my skin with the sandy powder from the bricks. Mother would give me a scolding for climbing on the bridge like this. She says the stones aren't as sturdy as they once were, and the last thing she wanted was a nasty accident.

Tucking a strand of my brunet waves under my flat cap, I swung myself around and landed on the bridge's safe side. I may have only been 13 years of age, but I did know my place: on the right side, where life was simple, where home was. I lived on the north end of town, where things were just about tolerable. My house wasn't too close to the back allies, where orphans and petty criminals often scuttled about, and the sweetshop was only a short walk away. My family may not have been the wealthiest, but in my neighbourhood, I was the closest thing to nobility they would ever get. As I got nearer to home, I took off my cap, dusted off my trousers and adjusted the belts strapped at my shoulders. Must look somewhat presentable for my stringent parents.

"Jacob, where have you been?" My mother embraced me.

"Where I always go every Sunday, mother. By Stone-Arch bridge."

She sighed, and looked over to my father who was smoking a pipe in his favourite armchair. He was contemplating things, it seemed.

"Jonah you tell him, tell him it's dangerous to be going all the way to the Southside of town just to dally on some old bridge."

My mother paused as my father got up.

"Whose son is he Rosie? My son, and he can hold his own."

My father approached me, ruffling my hair with a wistful grin.

"And besides, me and Marcel used to play there when we were lads, its plenty safe."

"Safe?" My mother croaked, in the process letting go of my strangled limbs.

My father, Jonah Lockhart, works as a doctor at a newly aspiring clinic and my mother, Rose Lockhart, works at the local hatters, sewing and selling bonnets for a living. I don't believe the career is fit for either of their skill sets, but I'm just a child, what do I know? While my parents debated, discussing something about 'allowing me to grow up', and other things like 'keeping me away from scum', I snuck up the stairs. As I mentioned, our home was 'tolerable'. We had a living room, a kitchen, three bedrooms and an outhouse. Why three bedrooms you ask? Well, one belonged to my parents, the other to me, and the last, for my uncle Marcel.

My uncle's room was in the attic, far from disturbances, far from the outside, far from... reality.

My father invited him here, apparently my grandparent's dying wish. His life had been shadowy, though he doesn't tell me why. All I know was he didn't marry, and his career didn't climb as high as he hoped. Despite the shadow that hungover the man, he paid me plenty of mind and answered most of my 'hows' and 'whys'.

"Uncle Marcel," I said while climbing the rickety stairs to the attic.

"Uncle Marcel, may I come in?" I knocked on the splintering hatch.

There was silence for some moments and then, without warning, a raspy, sing-song voice came from within-

"Not by the hairs of my chinny-chin chin!"

My face lit up, and suddenly I was filled with spirit.

"Then I'll huff, and I'll puff, and I'll"-

Before I could recite my drama, the wooden hatch opened, and two strong arms lifted me off my feet-

"Got you lad!"

Uncle Marcel held me, pulling me into a tight embrace. After spinning me around and making me view his room as if I were on a carnival ride, he fell back at his desk with a groan.

"Getting a bit heavy, ain't we?"

He plopped me at the edge of his knee, giving me a light-hearted smile. I smiled back, unsure how to respond to his jesting. I contemplated telling him that his hair was looking a bit dishevelled, or that there was an unsightly ink stain on his shirt, but perhaps that would be a little rude of me...

"Staring at the state I'm in, eh lad?" His gruff voice cut the atmosphere. Before I could protest, he started chuckling.

"Look here,"

Uncle Marcel opened up a little makeshift book and smacked his hand against a page filled to the brim with hurried writing, next to them were intricate sketches. There were drawings of various bits of attire, props, and many, many masks.

"I practice script writing daily, and sketch all the objects and attire my characters would need. Wishful thinking of course, it's not like I could put on a play of this kind without a theatre."

I furrowed my brows, considering my uncle's words...

"But uncle... why pursue something if you don't have all the resources?"

The man ruffled my hair, and sighed.

"Lad, pursuing something, even if that something seems unattainable, gives people like us purpose. And anyway, if you don't try, how will you know you can't succeed at it?"

I only half-understood what my uncle said, the part about trying. Despite my ignorance, I nodded. He returned the nod and, after broadening his eyes to the sight of his pocket watch, ushered me to bed. As I walked though his room, I paid close attention to the shelves filled with handcrafted props, and above the shelves, a wall pinned with clownish jester's masks. Hanging off his bed were drapes and cloth of plentiful colours, and scattered under his bed, were scrunched up balls of parchment. As I dropped through the hatch and closed it behind me, I thought more about what my uncle had said... what did he mean by 'unattainable' and 'people like us'? I carried these thoughts to bed with me, pondering whether he was referring to himself, or to society...

Closing notes

To all the readers who have made it this far. I sincerely hope you enjoyed reading my second book, *Through the Eyes of a Servant.* I loved creating this read so much that a sequel and a prequel is already in the making. Here's to meeting Thomas, Paula and the Ethel family again.

Priya Rohella
Author.

Portrait of the Jester created by Ritika
Rohella

Printed in Great Britain
by Amazon